Chapter 10…Confessions

A Miss Margaret Adventure #10

By L. G. Blankenship Diversion

Dedication

A true friend gives encouragement, love and forgiveness without being asked. They open their arms no matter what. I have found that friendship in a family that took me to be one of their own, giving me a smile and a hug when I need it the most, never telling me that I wasn't welcome and always, always showing me what real Christian love is. Thank you Minton family and thank you Lord, for leading me to this wonderful family.

Reviews! Reviews! Reviews!

Please take time to go back to Amazon and leave a review. Indie authors live by the reviews they acquire, for marketing, publishing, sales and postings. The more favorable reviews an author has on their work the faster they climb the long ladder to being a bestselling author and have a place in the top 100.

Chapter 1

We were all sitting nervously in the Sanctuary as the choir finishes the opening hymn. Where was Pastor Tom? The choir sits down, looking at the door, murmuring voices were wondering where the pastor was. Finally one of the deacons gets up and heads for the door to the hallway. Several minutes pass before the door opens and he reappears with Pastor Tom following. I let out the breath I had been holding.

After Tom got out of the hospital from being given the wrong medication, he had been acting a little strangely and today appears to be no exception. We wait as he stands at the pulpit looking out over the congregation, a look of confusion on his face.

Having enough I go to the podium, placing my hand over the microphone. "Tom, are you all right?"

He looks at me with confusion then recognition appears. "Margaret." He looks in front of him. "Oh my goodness." He waves me off. "I'm all right, thank you."

Returning to my seat, I carefully watch as he opens his Bible and smiles. "Good morning and isn't it a blessed one? Please join me as we delve into the passage of John 3:16." He opens his Bible then looks out over the congregation. "Today we learn that it isn't just us that depends on the love of God, of His forgiveness, of His everlasting compassion for His creatures. We know that the earth was made in six days with the Lord taking the seventh day as a day of rest. We know that when that ship was built, that two of every animal was taken aboard to be saved after the flood…"

I look at Max and frown, where was Tom going with this? Max looks over at Terry who also shrugs then glances at the congregation. It seems as if everyone was confused, after all John 3:16 was the verse on 'For God so loved the world that He gave His only begotten son, that whosoever believeth in Him will have everlasting life.' There was nothing there about the Ark, the animals or creating the earth in six days.

Tom rambles more but when he mentions David and Goliath. I lean toward Max and whisper. "I hate to say it but Tom has literally lost it."

Max nods at me then motions to the front where Tom was standing there, looking at his Bible with confusion on his face. "We need to get him out of here."

I get up and walk to the pulpit, laying a hand on top of his. "Tom." I say softly.

He slowly turns his head toward me with a look of confusion. "Margaret?"

"Tom, that was a good sermon, now let's go to your office." He nods as I lead him away from the pulpit and to the hallway doors. The congregation was quietly talking as I direct him through the door. Once we were on the other side, I stop him and look into his face. It was filled with confusion, his eyes looked blank.

Max joins me as I gently lead Tom down the hallway. "I've called Dr. Matthews, he'll meet us in the office." He follows us as we enter the office where Tom stops.

"Why are we here? I need to teach today. There's a classroom full of students waiting on me."

My heart was breaking to see my friend and
pastor having no idea where he was or what he was
doing. "No Tom, not today. We're waiting for a
friend to come see you."

Tom nods as we enter his office where he sits
down in one of the chairs that faces his desk. "When
will the Pope be here?"

Tears fill my eyes as I watch Tom look around
the office as if he had never seen it before.
"Soon."

A gentle hand touches my shoulder, I turn to
see Dr. Matthews standing beside Max with a look of
concern on his face. He motions for me to come with
him. Following him into the outer office, he asks,
"Margaret can you tell me what's happened?"

I explain how we had to get him to come to the
Sanctuary and then the confusion of the sermon,
adding lastly that he thought he was supposed to be
teaching a class. "Its dementia isn't it?"

Dr. Matthews shakes his head. "I'm not sure
yet, but I will say that the medication he was given
did have an adverse effect on his brain. I'd like to
admit him to the psych ward where we can run tests
and keep him under 24 hour surveillance." Tom had
been part of a scheme hatched by a family that was
taking revenge on any and everyone by replacing
their prescribed medications with drugs that worked
against their medical conditions.

"Oh my." My hands go to my cheeks as tears
fill my eyes. "Poor Tom."

Dr. Matthews nods then places an arm around my
shoulder. "It'll be all right Margaret. We just need
to find out what's going on. It could be as simple

as the medication hasn't left his system yet. Please don't give up on Tom."

Wiping at my eyes. "No I'm not. Do you need us to help you get him to the hospital?"

"Let's see if he remembers me first. He may come along willingly."

We re-enter Tom's office to hear him and Max talking about the fish that Tom had caught the day before and inviting us to dinner.

Dr. Matthews stands in front of Tom. "Hey Tom how are you?"

Tom looks up at Dr. Matthews, studying his face for a minute before smiling. "Hey Doc, you want to join us for a fish dinner?"

"Sure, but I'd like for you to come with me first, do you mind?"

Tom stands up. "Where are we going?"

Dr. Matthews puts an arm around Tom's shoulder. "I have a friend that I think needs some of your help."

Tom smiles. "Okay, let's go."

After they leave the office, I sit down in the chair that Tom had used. When I look over at my husband, the tears come fast and furious. He takes me in his arms, letting me cry the sadness out. "Oh Max."

Rubbing my arms. "Shhh, it'll be all right. Doc will find out what is going on." Kissing the top of my head. "I'm going to go tell everyone to go home. And no I'm not saying anything about what could be wrong, just that he's still recovering."

I nod and let Max go fill the congregation in on what was happening. Getting up I pull a couple of tissues out of the box on Tom's desk and blow my nose when I hear a throat clear. Turning around to see Terry and Tabitha standing in the doorway. "Mom what's going on with the pastor?"

"Oh sweetheart, we aren't sure yet."

Terry leans on the chair. "That was scary. Have you called the doctor?"

"Yes, Tom's with him now. He's going to admit Tom and run some tests on him. He's thinking the medicine Tom was given had an adverse effect on him and it may take more time to get out of his system."

Tabitha comes to put an arm around me. "It'll be all right Mom."

I nod into her shoulder as Terry joins us. "Maybe we could call a prayer meeting for him this afternoon."

Raising my head. "That's a good idea. Has everyone left yet?"

"No, everyone is still in the Sanctuary talking."

"Then let's go." Leading the way down the hallway to the Sanctuary to find Terry had been right, most everyone was still here.

I climb the steps to the pulpit, clearing my throat as I approach the podium. "Everyone. Please can I have your attention for a minute?" Everyone turns to face me. "As you know from this morning,

Tom isn't doing very well. He's with Dr. Matthews now and they are going to be running tests. But I would like to hold a prayer vigil for our pastor. Either we can all meet here again later this afternoon or leave the church open for people to come and pray all day. What do you think?"

Elsie, my friend, pops up. "Why not right now? Then people can come and go as they please the rest of the day."

I nod at her suggestion. "Good idea. If you don't mind I would like to start and then you can join in." I see a lot of nodding heads so I close my eyes and wait as the congregation gets quiet. Then let my heart tell me what to say. "Father we are here today to ask for Your healing touch to bless Pastor Tom with his memory and to heal him from the effects of the medicine he was given. We ask that Your servant can again take a place behind this pulpit delivering Your Word and message for us to hear. Lord, we ask that You help us understand, to guide us and direct us in helping Tom with his needs. Lord this we ask in Your name."

I stand with my hands clasped, concentrating on the Lord as someone else picks up the prayer. The Sanctuary fills with the Lord's Spirit as people pray for Tom and his healing, people cry as they speak for their beloved pastor. It was uplifting and when I open my eyes after the Amen, I see a room full of love, of friendship and family.

As I rejoin Max, he takes my hand and squeezes it while he talks with a couple of the deacons. Betty comes over with a crooked smile. "Margaret, should we be talking about finding someone to fill in for Tom while he's recovering?"

Oh, that thought had never entered my mind. "I hadn't thought of that. I guess we should because we have no idea how long Tom's going to be laid up." I think for a minute. "Let's see if we can have a meeting tomorrow afternoon. Since we're going to need someone next Sunday."

"All right. I'll call everyone tonight and we'll meet here. Thanks Margaret."

Well something else to be added on to our list of things to do.

Chapter 2

After we arrive home, I fix us all ham sandwiches with chips and iced tea. Joy was the first to remind me of something else we needed to think about. "Gram, I hate it about the pastor but know he's going to be fine. But this weekend is New Year's and then your first guest arrives. Don't we need to make sure everything is ready, you know, go to the store and all that?"

Dropping the half of sandwich that I was getting ready to bite into and look over at Max, who was smirking. "Well let's just add more to the list. I think we have the room ready. We just need to put sheets on the bed and make sure the bathroom is ready. But yes, we definitely need to go to the store."

"If you make a list Tabitha and I can take care of that." Terry had already finished his first sandwich and was working on another.

"Thank you. Do we want to do anything for New Years, or do you two have plans?"

Joy answers for Terry. "Mom and Terry want to have a get together of all the workers, I think they have a bonus for them all."

Tabitha drops her chip. "And how did you know that?"

Joy smiles, "I'm your daughter ma, I can read you like a book. Plus the fact you aren't very quiet sometimes when you talk."

"Well great. Does anyone else know about this?"

Joy shakes her head. "I may know but I wouldn't tell anyone and spoil the surprise."

Tabitha lets a breath out. "Thank goodness." She turns to me. "If you want to have dinner together before we go to the plant will be fine."

Max looks at me and smiles. "Tell you what, you two do your thing and Maggie and I will have our first New Years here alone."

All three of the kids smile, with Joy giving Max a wink. "Uh- huh, you just want Grams all to yourself."

"As a matter of fact, I do. A quiet meal, maybe a good movie and at midnight a dance with my special lady." He takes my hand and kisses my knuckles.

Blushing, I look over at my daughter to see her trying not to smile too much, but Joy doesn't have that problem, she laughs before saying. "Way to go Max!"

Oh my, now to get the subject changed. "I need one of you men to go to the basement and make sure everything down there is set. We need to get all the laundry done, oh and get the TV for that room hooked up."

Terry wipes his hands. "I can do the TV and we can check out the basement for you then you give us the list and we'll take care of going to the store. That way you'll have time to spend with Tom and to handle things at church if you need to."

My heart swells. "Thank you Terry."

With my to-do list a lot smaller than it was, I go to the little desk we had in the foyer to find out exactly when our first guests were to arrive. The Carson's were scheduled to arrive two days after New Year's Day so a little less than a week. Oh so exciting!

I read the little that Mary Ann had noted about the couple. They were retired and visiting each state that their family had ties too. That was interesting. They wanted a king size bed if possible, which it was and had requested a smoking room. Oh my. Well if they were smokers they would have to go outside. I would put some kind of container on one of the tables on the patio for them.

After seeing if there was anything else they needed, I went upstairs to check out the room they would be staying in. Opening the door at the end of the hallway, I find the room ready except for the TV. The small refrigerator was even stocked with snacks and drinks.

Satisfied that there was nothing else that needed to be done, I leave the room and head for my bedroom to find the cats were in their usual places on the pillows.

Changing into slacks and a blouse before going back downstairs to clean the kitchen, I find Max and Terry unpacking the TV with a pile of cables around their feet. Leaving them to their work, I start washing the few dishes we had used and putting the sandwich makings back in the refrigerator. Once I had the kitchen clean again, I recheck on the men only to find them gone then I hear a loud bang from upstairs and knew they were working in the guest room.

In the den, I straighten the blanket and toss it on the back of the couch then head for the desk and the outline for the procedure of finding a pastor.

As I think of that, I wonder how Tom was doing, so I find my cell phone and call Dr. Matthews to see if he can give me an update but I get his voice mail. After leaving a message, I take the papers and put them beside my bag on the kitchen counter then pick my Bible up and head for the patio. It won't be much longer that we can enjoy it out here. We were having a warmer than normal winter so far and I was taking advantage of it.

Turning my face to the sun, I close my eyes and let the sun's rays warm my face. My mind turns to Tom and what was happening to him. Dementia was a terrible thing and I was praying that it wasn't that, but effects from him being given the wrong medication, which hopefully could be fixed. As I ponder this my cell dings, looking at the screen there was a text from Dr. Matthews telling me that Tom was sleeping comfortably and had a few moments of clarity when he got to the hospital. It seems he was aware that something was wrong and willing to do whatever it took to get better.

Closing my eyes again I pray for Tom, for Dr. Matthews and for there to be a cure, but if not, that Tom would be comfortable. Picking my Bible up I hold it for a moment, the verse that Tom quoted this morning, John 16:3, 'For God so loved the world that he gave his only begotten son, that whosoever believeth in him will have everlasting life.'

Always one of my favorite verses, it made a promise that each person that believed would live forever, maybe not on earth but in Heaven with the

Father. How overwhelming to know that you were loved that much!

My eyes close as I hold my Bible and visualize being in heaven with the Father and Son and every living creature.

Chapter 3

Feeling a hand rubbing my cheek, I open my eyes to see Max standing over me smiling. "So why the rest of us are tangling with a huge TV, you're down here taking a nap in the sun."

Sitting up and laying my Bible down, I smile at my husband. "As a matter of fact, yes."

Max sets down two glasses filled with ice and coke before taking a chair. "Must be nice. What time is your meeting tonight?"

Glancing at my watch I see that it's almost five, "At six thirty. Do you want something to eat before I leave?"

Max has his head leaned back with his eyes closed. "No I don't think so. If I get hungry I'll just fix a sandwich."

"Did you get the TV mounted on the wall?"

"We did and it's working so that's off the list. Terry and Tabitha have gone to the store so that will be done. Can you think of anything else?"

"I saw on the reservation that they smoke so we need to make a place out here for them because they are not smoking in the house." I tap the table to make my point.

"No they're not. I think there's an old large ceramic pot in the shed. We can fill that with wet sand for them to use."

"Fine we'll use that and move that table over to the far edge of the patio for them." I think for a minute. "Then put no smoking signs all over the house and make sure they know they can't do it anywhere but at that table. I'd hate to find cigarette butts in the fish pond or in the flower beds."

"Maybe we should just say no smoking on the premises."

"Good idea. I'll have Joy add it to the website."

We both get quiet and enjoy this rare warm December day. Max takes my hand and squeezes it before getting up. "I hear a car."

Joining him, we walk around the side of the house to see Terry and Tabitha pulling bags out of the trunk of their car. We each grab a handful and walk into the kitchen, once all the bags were unloaded I look around. "My goodness I had no idea the list had this much food on it. We may need to build another pantry."

Max smiles as he starts to unload the bags. "We'll be fine. But I think you need to get to your meeting. We'll get all this put away."

Looking at the clock, I almost gasp, where had the time gone, besides taking a nap under the sun? Jogging up the stairs, I wash my face and run a brush through my hair before heading back downstairs. Picking up my bag and the papers, I kiss Max and the kids before leaving the house and getting into my little red bug.

Pulling into the church parking lot to see that most everyone was already here. In the church, I head for the conference room to find Betty fixing a pot of coffee and opening a box of cookies from the bakery. "Hello Betty. Can I help?"

Turning to face me with a smile. "Hey Margaret, no I think that's it. Have you heard anything about Tom?"

"Yes, he's resting and it sounds as if Dr. Matthews is optimistic on his recovery."

"That's good news." She takes a seat at the side of the table and I sit across from her.

Slowly the others start coming in and none of them seemed thrilled to be here.

Betty brings the meeting to order. "All right what we are looking for is someone that can carry on Tom's duties while he's recovering."

"Well let's not get the pastor we had last time. He was quite gruff." Rob Murphy wasn't one to mince words.

The others nod their heads at his statement, including Betty. "I was able to get a list of the available interim pastors today and there aren't very many in the area to choose from. But there is a young pastor that has moved to the area and looking for a church. He's willing to be an interim until he's placed."

She hands out a paper that introduces the pastor. As I read his resume and the recommendation of the pastor search board, I was impressed, then I look at his picture. He was young, much younger than we were used to, but he had a pleasant face. The picture was in black and white but it seemed he had brown hair cut short and light colored eyes, I smile at the dimple in his chin. His name was Ross Gillen, married with three children.

His resume was impressive and I had a very good feeling about him. Looking up to see that everyone was studying his information, I wait until they finish before saying anything. "I like this one." I slide the paper to the middle of the table. "He comes highly recommended, has a family and is looking for an established church that has strong community ties." I look up and smile. "Ours can't be much stronger."

I hear a couple of chuckles since this was one of the first churches that had been built in the area. And not to brag but one of the best too, since my family had started the church.

Betty looks around the table. "All right, let's take a vote. All those in favor of Pastor Ross Gillen raise their hands." Everyone but Mrs. Hopkins raised their hands, so he was going to be our new interim. "Good. Well that's done. I'll contact the office tomorrow and see if they can ask the pastor to come visit with us before Sunday and if we approve, he'll be the one. Any questions?"

Mrs. Hopkins raises her hand. "Yes I didn't agree so why are you voting him in?"

Betty sighs, because dealing with Mrs. Hopkins was more than a chore. "Because there was a majority vote, you were the only one against."

"Yes and I don't think we need a pastor that appears to be right out of high school. I think we should get Hugh back and be done with it."

Betty closes her eyes and I ask softly. "Want me to answer?" Betty nods at me. Turning to Mrs. Hopkins. "We appreciate your input but the majority rules. And we had quite a few complaints the last time that Hugh was in the pulpit."

"Well I didn't complain so that should mean something. I don't like this young man." She slides the paper to the middle of the table.

"Do you know something about him that we don't because unless you know him, you have no idea what he's like, so how can you say you don't like him?" I hated to admit she sounded like the way I used to be.

"Look at that picture! He's what eighteen? There is no way that man can be a preacher and I'm flat against him." She glares at me.

"All right. We know how you feel, but the other eight of us have voted yes so that's it." I turn to Mrs. Hopkins. "And after he does preach and you find you do like him, I would like to hear an apology." I turn to Betty, "Would you like to close the meeting? I believe we're done."

"Margaret Bishop, one of these days you are going to get your comeuppance!" Mrs. Hopkins points her finger at me before grabbing her bag and leaving the room.

I look at everyone. "If that was the way I was, I deeply apologize."

That seemed to break the ice some and I got a few smiles and heard a couple of Amen's as we broke up the meeting. Betty holds my arm as I start to leave. Turning to her, she says, "How can we get her off the committee? Every time we have a meeting she stirs up some kind of trouble."

"I understand. It wasn't that long ago I was the same way. The only thing I can think of is to find something that she's passionate about. She used to be a wonderful Sunday School teacher but that was taken away from her, maybe we should try that again."

"Good idea. Let me think on that for a while and thank you for taking over."

We say good night and make sure the lights were out in the church and the door secure as we leave.

On the drive home, I say a prayer for Mrs. Hopkins then make a mental note to pay her a visit, I was sure there was something more going on.

Chapter 4

Back at the mansion, I find it quiet. Terry and Tabitha had left, the kitchen was in order even though the refrigerator was completely packed as was the pantry. And Max was in the den, his feet on the coffee table, the remote in his hand and sound asleep.

Oscar and Felix were curled around his legs, barely opening their eyes when I walk in the room. "Well good evening to you too." Rubbing their heads, I get some purrs before they close their eyes and go back to sleep.

Deciding it was a good time to soak in a hot bath, I go upstairs taking a detour to the guest room at the end of the hall. Opening the door, I smile. The TV was mounted on the wall opposite of the bed and everything else was in place and ready for our first guests. Thinking I would enjoy staying in a room this nice, I shut the door and head to the other end of the hallway to our room.

In the bathroom, I fill the tub with hot water and bubbles before washing my face. After soaking until the water starts getting chilly, I get into my warm pajamas then slather cream on my hands and face. In the bedroom, I take the cat's pillows off the bed before pulling the covers down and sliding into bed. Picking my Bible up, I prop myself against the headboard then let the Bible fall open where it may. My eyes land on Proverbs 13, so I start reading at verse 1. A wise child loves discipline but a scoffer does not listen to rebuke. From the fruit of their words good persons eat good things, but the desire of the treacherous is for wrongdoing. Those who guard their mouths preserve their lives, this who open wide their lips come to ruin.

Oh my, this could be about Mrs. Hopkins so I close my Bible and pray for her, for Tom, for the pastor we were looking at and for our new venture into being an inn, as I finish Max comes into the room with two cats following him.

"How did the meeting go?" Max asks as he climbs into bed.

"Well we have a candidate that Mrs. Hopkins strongly voiced her opinion on even though it was a unanimous vote except for her. She wants Hugh back."

Max turns to me with a frown. "Hugh! The man couldn't stay on track and he complained when someone coughed or sneezed and let's not even mention what he said when the Collins' baby cried. No, I wouldn't agree to that." He shakes the covers a little more than necessary which made Oscar growl at him before moving to my side of the bed.

"We talked to her, but I think I'll go visit her. For some reason I think there's more going on with her." I lean over to give my husband a kiss good night. "Only four more days and we'll officially be an inn!"

He smiles at me as he takes my hand and kisses it. "Yes we will. It will be an adjustment and I think we need to add a TV in here too. What if we have guests and I want to watch a game. You know I usually fall asleep before it's over."

I look at the wall opposite our bed which had the French doors that led to the balcony then to the wall where the dresser was. "Maybe we can put one on the dresser for now."

Max looks at the room. "We can hang one in the corner there. That way it'll be out of the way and I can see it fine from here."

Nodding at his suggestion. "All right. Do you want me to pick one up tomorrow?"

"If you don't mind. I have a meeting with the two new officers tomorrow." He pulls the covers up and turns the light on his side of the bed off. Taking my hand, we thank God for our day and for protection during the night and for Mrs. Hopkins.

"Good night Mrs. Gunderson." Max smiles as he gives me a light kiss.

"And to you Mr. Gunderson." I turn my light off and slide down under the covers letting the cats decide where they were going to sleep before closing my eyes.

Chapter 5

I wake the next morning to two cats digging their little paws into my side. Rolling over I take both in my arms, "Are we hungry and where has my husband gone to?" I get a soft yeow from Felix as Oscar licks my chin. "Okay kitties let's get dressed and go get something to eat and a cup of coffee for me." Seeing as the cats understood English, they jump off the bed as I throw the covers back.

Getting up, I open the drapes over the French doors and smile at the clear sky and bright sunshine. "Good morning Lord." With the smile still on my face, I head for the bathroom to get ready for the day. I think about what I had to do, as to what I was going to put on.

I had every intention of visiting Mrs. Hopkins and then needed to pick another TV up. I also needed to drop by the courthouse and pick our license up since it had to be displayed in the inn. Other than that I think my day was clear.

After dressing in jeans and a long sleeved shirt I head downstairs to find Max at the kitchen table with the paper and an empty cup and plate. Reaching him I place my hands on his shoulders before leaning down and kissing his cheek. "Good morning my dear husband."

Turning his face so that he could kiss my lips, "And to you my lovely wife."

Picking his empty cup up, I refill it before filling my own cup and carrying them both to the table. Sitting down I ask. "And what are you doing today besides meeting with the new officers?"

"Depends on if anything has happened overnight. Other than that, I'm hoping for a quiet day. And what are your plans?"

"Maybe visit Mrs. Hopkins, pick a TV up and drop by to get the license." I gaze out the window at the backyard and notice that there was actually a daffodil blooming beside the patio. The weather had been unseasonably warm lately, but really.

"You know maybe I should get the TV, there's no way you can get it in the VW."

Turning to my thoughtful husband. "Good idea. Okay so you get the TV which leaves me more free time today." I smile at him which makes him laugh.

"That was either shrewd or I'm a really nice guy." Folding the paper, he gets up then leans down, pecking me on the nose. "And I'm going to say shrewd. See you later."

After he leaves I feed the cats then fix a bowl of cereal, since I really wasn't very hungry. Finishing, I clean the dishes Max had used and mine then wipe everything down in the kitchen before going into the den to straighten up. Putting the blanket back on the couch and opening the drapes, I go to the desk and look at the pictures of the Cambridge's that I had on the wall, hoping they would be all right with the decision we had made on making the mansion an inn.

Pulling the picture album out, I set it on the desk and open it carefully. Turning each page, I gaze at the few images that were left of the family that had built the mansion and a few of the surrounding buildings along with having an award winning rose named after them.

Turning a page I noticed that two pages were stuck together, carefully I pry them apart. Why hadn't I noticed this before? On the page was a photo of another couple, a distinguished man who was smiling along with a plain woman that wasn't smiling. Under the photo was some writing but I couldn't make it out. Carrying the album to the window, I let the sun shine on the page. Squinting I could barely make out the name but it looked like Carson or maybe Carlisle or it could be Carter. Giving up I put the album back on the shelf before heading to the kitchen.

Looking around to find my keys were on the table instead of beside the phone where I usually kept them and think from now on we'd have to put things like this up and out of sight. Grabbing my bag I head to the garage and my little red bug.

Pulling out of the garage, I decide this was a good day to put the top down, so with the wind tossing my short hair, I head to town. As I drove I think of how to approach Mrs. Hopkins and decide that honestly and straightforward would be the best way.

I stop at the courthouse first, finding a parking place on the street, I put the top up on my car before getting out and walking across the street. Entering the courthouse, I go to the clerk's office, seeing Tina Clemmons working the counter. "Good morning Tina."

"Why Mrs. Gunderson how are you?"

"Fine, thank you. I'm here to pick up our license for the inn."

She turns away to pull a file off a desk behind her. "Oh yes, it came in several days ago. Just sign this page and you're in business."

Taking the page from her, I sign my name and date it then hand it back. She makes a copy, handing that along with the license to me. "Thank you. I guess we're official now?" With a smile I leave the courthouse.

Waiting for a couple of cars to pass before I cross the street, I hear my name being called. Turning, I see Elsie waving at me frantically. "Maggie! Maggie"

Waiting for Elsie to catch up to me. "Good morning Elsie, what brings you out so early?"

Stopping to catch her breath. "Oh!" She leans over and places her hands on her knees. Finally she straightens up. "Did you hear?"

"Hear what?"

"About Mrs. Hopkins?"

My stomach took a nose dive. "No, what about Mrs. Hopkins?"

Fanning her face with her hand. "Oh my." She takes a deep breath before speaking again. "A neighbor noticed her front door open and when they went to check they found her in the hallway, dead."

Chapter 6

Staring at Elsie as she takes her hat off and fans her face. "Yes they said she was all blue and everything. Oh I wish I had seen that."

"Elsie!" I motion to the bench so we could sit down to talk. "Now tell me what you know." Because she usually knew more than what happened, always adding her own speculations.

"Well, like I said the neighbor went in and found her on the floor. From what she said it looked as if she just walked in the house and fell down. Maybe she had a massive heart attack or a stroke, maybe there was someone in the house and hit her or maybe strangled her. There wasn't any blood so they couldn't have shot her or stabbed her and they probably didn't have time to poison her."

"Elsie." It took a moment to get her attention. "What was she wearing, do you know?"

"Wearing? Well I guess a dress, she always wore those long dresses like you used to."

"So you don't know?"

"Why is that important?"

"When we had our meeting last night, she was in a mood. A not very pleasant mood, she wanted to argue and she got a little mad. So I was thinking by the time she got home she was probably furious and maybe had a heart attack. If she was wearing a blue printed dress with a lace collar and carrying a handkerchief, then this must have happened right after our meeting."

"Oh." A smile brightens her face. "I can find
out." Taking her cell phone out of her bag, she
punches in a number. "Cornelia, this is Elsie. You
said you found Mrs. Hopkins, do you remember what
she was wearing? Was it a blue printed dress?" Elsie
looks at me and nods. "Thanks. We may have a time of
death down." Pressing the screen on the phone again,
she looks at me and smiles. "Yes a blue printed
dress, so you're thinking she croaked right after
your meeting."

I sigh. "We really need to talk about your
choice of words but yes, I do believe this happened
last night." Pulling my own cell phone out, I call
Max. "Hello dear, I just heard about Mrs. Hopkins,
if she was wearing a blue print dress with a lace
collar, that's what she was wearing at the meeting
last night, so this must have happened as soon as
she got home and she was in a foul mood."

"I'll have to check on her clothing, but the
ME has placed the TOD at between 6 and 8 last
evening. You said she was upset about the decision
you made, so it may have caused a heart attack. Let
me call downstairs and tell them. Thanks Maggie."

Tucking my phone back in my bag, I turn back
to Elsie. "He's going to check but the time of death
is about right."

"So you've already figured this one out. What
a bummer, I was hoping for a culprit to hunt down."

"I feel awful."

"Why? You didn't kill her."

"No, but if she hadn't gotten so angry at the
meeting she may not have had a heart attack, if

that's what happened." Getting up I add, "I was going to visit her today."

Elsie pushes herself up. "You can't blame yourself for her temper. She must have had some health problems if just getting a little upset caused a heart attack."

Even though Elsie had a mouth on her, she always came through as a friend, sometimes saying the right thing at the right moment. Smiling at her, "Thanks Elsie. I needed to hear that." We hug goodbye and I get into my car and sit for a minute, thinking. Still feeling a little sad about Mrs. Hopkins, I knew that Elsie was right, I couldn't blame myself but that was hard to do.

Sighing, I start the car and wonder what to do with my day now. I had the license, Max was picking up the TV and I couldn't visit Mrs. Hopkins now. The house was clean, the laundry was caught up, definitely didn't need anything from the store.

I pull away from the curb and head to the other side of town and the library. When we were researching the Cambridge's we had found a treasure trove of information of the town during that period, maybe I could find something about the photo I had found in the album.

Pulling into the parking lot, which was almost full, I smile. Most libraries were having a difficult time since most people were reading their books digitally now, but not here.

Entering the library to a low murmur of people talking, I go to the counter and smile at the clerk. I didn't know the young girl but her nametag read Patricia. "Hello. I was wondering if I could look in

the archives. Maybe from the years 1890 to around
1950."

Giving me a strange look, the clerk nods
toward the room that held the microfiche. "Seems as
if you may know where they are, so you can help
yourself." She studies me a little more. "Are you
Margaret? The chief's wife?"

"Yes I am."

A huge smiles lights her face up, "So cool!
I've been wanting to meet you. My boyfriend is an
officer and he talks about you a lot. Says you have
a knack for figuring things out. He's really
impressed by you."

I could feel the blood rushing to my face. "Oh
my, that is quite a compliment. Who is tour
boyfriend?"

"Eric Spence, he hasn't been on the force
long, but he says that you usually are on the
toughest cases."

"Please thank him for me and it was nice
meeting you." Still feeling the heat on my face, I
go into the room and shut the door behind me.
Pulling a chair out from underneath the table, I
turn the microfiche machine on then look in the
files for the years I wanted. The library had put
all the newspapers on microfiche several years ago,
which I was thankful for, it made looking for things
a lot easier.

Chapter 7

Two hours later I had found a photo of the Cambridge's with a group of people dedicating the new wing of the clinic. The caption mentioned a couple named James and Mary Carson and it was the couple in the photo, there was no mistaking the chin on James Carson. Carson? Why did that sound familiar? Oh, our first guests, the Carson's!"

I read through the article and go through a couple more years until I come to the obituary of Mary Carson. She had died from the flu and I noticed several other obituaries had deaths blamed on the flu. Of course that was before the flu shot and most of the effective antibiotics. Such a shame.

So maybe our guests were distance relatives of the Carson's. That would be another chapter to the history of the mansion. Maybe the newspaper would like to interview them on their family history.

Putting the files back and turning the machine off, I leave the room to see that a meeting of some sort was taking place in the main room. From the people I see, I was thinking it was a meeting of the hospital board, smiling at a few of the people as I pass them.

Back in my car I wonder what to do with the rest of my day then decide that I would try to visit Pastor Tom. Heading in the direction of the hospital, I take a quick detour into a fast food restaurant and go through the drive thru, ordering a hamburger meal with a chocolate shake.

Parking the car at the back of the lot after I had my food, I say a prayer of blessing before reaching into the bag and pulling the hamburger out.

Taking a deep breath before removing the wrapper and taking a bite, I close my eyes, it was so good!

As I eat, I watch the street in front of me, the drugstore now had a new window and it seems as if Hal may have had the building washed too. The traffic going in and out of the store was a promising sign that business for him was booming and for that I was glad, especially after the debacle with the wrong medications being given to a few people, all for revenge of sorts. Unfortunately Tom had been one of those people.

Finishing my meal, I head for the hospital and park in the front lot. Checking my hair in the rearview mirror to make sure it wasn't blown all over the place before opening the door.

Asking at the desk what room Tom was in, I see Dr. Matthews walking down the hallway. When he sees me he smiles. "Margaret, good to see you. Are you here to visit with Tom?"

"If that's all right, yes I would like to see him."

He turns with me and we walk down the hallway. "He's doing well. He's remembering people now. He's also eating well, which is good." Stopping in front of a door. "Just be yourself." He opens the door for me.

Entering the room to find Tom sitting in a chair watching TV, when he sees me he smiles. "Maggie!" Pushing himself up, he walks over to me for a hug, but I notice he has trouble putting one foot in front of the other.

I look over at Dr. Matthews who just nods at me. "I'll let you two have a visit. Tom I'll check

back on you in a bit. Margaret always a pleasure."
He pulls the door shut behind him.

Finally reaching me, Tom gives me a tight hug
before climbing back onto the bed. "How are you
Maggie?"

Sitting down in the one chair in the room, I
smile at Tom. "I'm fine, but more importantly how
are you?"

Tom frowns. "I guess I have my moments. Doc
says I'm doing well and that it shouldn't take very
long for that medicine to get out of my system
totally. Then hopefully I'll be back in the pulpit."

"Yes let's pray that happens." I thought maybe
we should get his mind on something besides what he
was here for. "Have you ever met a pastor by the
name of Ross Gillen?"

Tom's face scrunches as he thinks. "For some
reason the name sounds familiar but I don't know
why."

"We may use him until you get well and I
thought you may have heard of him."

Tom looks at me with a frown, I could tell he
was concentrating hard. "Young man, has a family. I
don't think he's been out of seminary long but I
heard him preach when he was before the board for
interim pastor. He's good, very good."

"Then you approve of him while you're
recovering? You don't want us to use Hugh again?" I
knew I'd probably just lit a fire, but I wanted to
see a little brimstone in Tom about now.

Tom looks at me. "I do, I think he'd be a good fit and no, after the last time Hugh was there, I heard more complaints than taking a vacation would be worth." He turns his head, "Hugh, what a joke. Complaining about someone sneezing."

I let him talk to himself for a minute. "Is there anything I can get you or do for you?"

"Baby." He raises his eyebrows at me.

"Your cat! Of course, I'll run by and get her on my way home." I smack my own forehead. "Why didn't I think of that?"

"I would appreciate it. Her food is in the cabinet beside the stove and you know where her blanket is. Poor thing probably thinks I've abandoned her."

"If they let animals in to visit, I would bring her by for you."

He gives me a little laugh, then lays his head back against the pillow.

I let him rest for a minute then I gently touch his arm. "Tom, Tom?"

His head jerks up and he looks at me. He frowns, "Can I help you?"

Okay, so his memory still comes and goes. "No I was just checking on you. Have a good nap."

Closing his eyes again, I say a quiet prayer for his healing before leaving the room.

Chapter 8

With a purpose now, I head for Tom's house to pick up his cat, Baby. We've kept her before, so my cats accept her as one of their own and Max adores her.

Pulling into the driveway of Tom's house, I park and head for the flower pot that had the key hidden in it. Reaching into the pot, I find the key and head for the back door, seeing Baby sitting in the kitchen window. With a smile I unlock the door and Baby is immediately rubbing my legs. Reaching down, I pick her up and cuddle her to my chest. "I'm sorry Baby girl, you're going to have to come home with me again."

Still holding Baby, I walk through the house, checking to make sure all the doors and windows were shut and locked. Back in the kitchen I let Baby down while I gather her food, treats and toys. Putting everything into a bag, I gather Baby up and put her in her carrier then shut the house up.

Setting the carrier in the front seat, I get in and turn my car around, heading for home with Baby expressing her displeasure the whole way.

Back at the mansion, I gather Baby and her things then go inside. "Oscar, Felix come see who's going to visit for a while." Hearing them before they enter the kitchen to see me taking Baby out of the carrier. Felix is the first to come and welcome her back, while Oscar sits in the doorway with his trademark glare. "Okay Oscar the glare doesn't work, we all know you like Baby. Now make nice." Oscar gives me his 'you have got to be kidding' look before turning around with a swish if his tail and leaves the room. "Grouch."

Tucking Baby's food away then putting her things in the den, I go to the little desk in the alcove and look up the reservation list. The Carson's will be here in four days, staying an entire week. I pull up their reservation form. They presently live in Connecticut and were going to be here for pleasure. Neither one listed a job, matter of fact there was very little information on either of them.

Checking the other reservations that would be here the following week, two couples were both here for two nights and they stated they were here for pleasure also.

Well that was a dead end, but if they were related to the Carson's that were in the photo with the Cambridge's, they may be here to find relatives. That would be interesting.

The house phone rings and I answer with the name of the inn. "Hello, I'd like to see if I could make a reservation for a week from now. We'd like to stay two days if possible."

Opening the calendar on the computer. "Let me check for you to see what we have available. I see we have a double room with a shared both at that time. Will that work for you?"

"That'll be fine. We're just stopping on our way south and thought seeing the Blue Ridge Mountains for a couple of days would be relaxing."

"Yes the mountains are beautiful year round and there are several trails open if you like to hike. Now there will be two of you for two nights. Can I have your name please?"

"Oh sorry. That would be Robert and Jill Carson."

I stop entering the data. "I'm sorry you said Carson?"

"Yes, that's right."

I take a breath. "Okay I have you down and you can check in anytime after 11 am. I'm sorry but we don't have a breakfast service available."

"Oh that's no problem, we'll be browsing through the town anyway. See you then."

They hang up and I sit there. That is not a coincidence for two couples having the same name staying here at the same time. Were they looking for something, or just vacationing? Something was telling me that this was more than just passing through.

My cell phone rings this time, checking the display to see it was Betty calling. "Hello Betty."

"Margaret. I was able to get in touch with Ross Gillen and he is eager to talk with us, so I made an appointment tomorrow at 10am, does that word with you?"

"Yes. I visited Tom today and he is pleased that we're considering Ross Gillen, he said he was a bright young man and delivers a wonderful sermon, oh he also said to not get Hugh again."

Betty laughs. "I can understand that. Isn't it terrible about Mrs. Hopkins? Have you heard anything?"

"Yes it is and I'm sorry the only thing I know, is it could be a heart attack or stroke."

"I know this sounds cruel and heartless, but I hope so. At least that way it was a natural death and not a murder. Thanks Margaret, I'll see you tomorrow."

Ending the call with Betty, my mind starts wondering and I make a mental note to ask Max when he got home what they thought the cause of death was.

Speaking of him, I hear the back door open and his voice. "Maggie you home? Well look who's here. Hi Baby girl."

When I enter the kitchen, I see Max holding Baby to his chest. "I see you found our guest."

"Did you visit Tom today?"

"I did and he was coherent most of the visit."

"That's good news. What did the doc say?" Baby had made herself quite at home in his arms.

I sit down at the table. "He's optimistic, he thinks once all of the old medication is out of his system, he should make a recovery."

"More good news." He sits down still holding Baby who was eating it up.

"Oh. We have more reservations, another couple next week. Max we have two couples with the name of Carson coming at the same time. That can't be a coincidence."

Max looks at me and raises an eyebrow. "No it can't. Any ideas?"

Chapter 9

Tapping my chin, I start to explain my thinking. "I found an old photo of the Cambridge's and another couple. I couldn't make the name out on the back, but I went to the library and looked at some old articles. There was a photo of several couples that were involved in the clinic, the Cambridge's and the Carson's. Both couples that made reservations are named Carson." I watch his face to see what he was thinking.

After several minutes, he looks at me. "Can you find anything out about the Carson's?"

"I haven't really looked. But I will now, it's just too convenient and I don't have a good feeling about it." I think of how I should start when Mrs. Hopkins crosses my mind. "Can you tell me anything about Mrs. Hopkins?"

"As of right now, it looks to be natural causes, once the autopsy is done we'll know for sure. There wasn't any indication of a break in and there was nothing missing as far as we can tell. She didn't have any family and apparently no close friends so there's no one to confirm that."

I think on that for a second. "No, Elsie has been there and so have the prayer group. They may not have gone further than the kitchen and living room, but that may be something."

Gently putting Baby on the floor, Max gets up. "Can you get in touch with them and ask them to call me?"

I nod as Max gives me a kiss on the forehead. "See you in a little while." Then with a smile, "Do

I need to pick anything up for dinner or is there enough here?"

Smacking at him as he laughs and steps out of the way. Once he was gone, I get my laptop and set it up on the kitchen table. I needed to see what I could find out about the Carson's. Going to the little desk I get both couples names and head back to my laptop.

Terry and Joy had shown me several sites I could go to and enter legally to find out information about just about anyone. Entering the first couple's name, dozens of articles came up. They were philanthropists, besides what they had done here in River Oaks, it appears they had given to several organizations across the country. I found the same photo I had seen at the library, there was a link under it so I click on it which takes me to another site. When the site opens I gasp, it was on unsolved crimes. I read through the first page to find out that the Carson's had vanished suddenly, leaving their home and all their belongings. Foul play had always been considered, but there was no evidence to prove or disclaim it. Hum.

I read through a few more articles and then type in the other names. Not as much on them until I find another photo with a link, this time an article comes up questioning whether the claim that Robert Carson was really the son of the original Carson since there were never any children born to them according to birth records and distant relatives. Well that was interesting.

Having a thought, I go to the town's public site and look at the property records of the mansion. There was never any question on the ownership since it was built of belonging to the

Cambridge's, but I wanted to see if any other name came up anywhere and it didn't. So I enter the name Carson and wait as the page loads. There had been four families in River Oaks by the name Carson. Three had been original families of the town, so they were gone before the Cambridge's had arrived and there were no property records for them, only rental information where they lived at the old mines housing. The last couple appeared to own property on the same road as the mansion, but besides our home and Noah's, there were only two other houses and they were fairly new. Of course the road led all the way to the top of the mountain, but I don't ever remember seeing any other buildings.

Maybe Noah would know, I'll have to ask him if there's anything further up the road.

Glancing at the clock, I had been on the laptop for three hours. Max will be home anytime wanting dinner. Shutting down the computer, I tuck it away before opening the refrigerator and groan. "This is ridiculous to have this much food in the house." Seeing a pack of pork chops, some fresh broccoli and corn, I decide that would work fine.

Pulling the food out, I put the broccoli in the steamer then shuck the corn and slather some butter on it before rolling foil over the cobs and putting them in the oven. Pulling a skillet out, I pour a little oil on the bottom then add a little crushed pepper and sea salt.

Wiping my hands on a towel, I turn to see three pairs of eyes looking at me. "Just have to go into the kitchen and you think it's time to eat." Not even getting a yeow. "All right, I give." Filling all three cats' bowls, I set them down and watch Baby and Felix as they start devouring their food as Oscar slowly sniffs his before taking a bite and deciding it was good.

After setting the table, then checking the corn, I head for the den to see if there was anything on the news. But before I take a step out of the kitchen, the back door opens. "Hello Chief. Any news on Mrs. Hopkins?"

Wrapping an arm around my waist, "As a matter of fact," Giving me a kiss before sitting down at the table to take his boots off. "It was a heart attack," He looks at me. "But not a natural heart attack. It seems there was an overload of insulin and a puncture mark below her left ear."

I plop down in a chair. "Who would want her dead?"

Max looks at me. "We've just started the investigation." He takes my hand. "Is there any way I can ask you not to get involved?"

Giving my husband a look that asks, do you even know me, then shake my head. "Probably not. I can talk to the prayer group and I know her hairdresser and that she liked to go to the diner on Mondays…"

Max holds his hand up. "Never mind." Then he points a finger at me. "But you be careful. After finding you in the basement of the drugstore, I'd prefer you to stay out of things but I know I'm wasting my breath." Taking my hand. "Be careful please."

"Of course." I pat his cheek. "Hungry?"

Chapter 10

As I finish fixing dinner, the back door opens and Noah walks in. "Maggie."

"Hello Noah. Oh I wonder if you could go with me up the mountain road." I relay what I had found out on the Carson's and why. "So I was thinking we could investigate a little unless you know of any houses that used to be there."

"Only the cabin and that was my uncles. But we can look." He looks at the food I was preparing. "I didn't mean to interrupt your dinner but I wanted to talk to Max for a minute." He turns and walks over to where Max was glancing at the newspaper. I couldn't hear what they were saying but they both walk out of the room. Hum.

Just as I finish dinner and set it on the table, the men come back in, neither one looking very pleased. "Noah we have plenty if you'd like to stay."

Noah glances at the table then smiles. "That would be nice. Thank you." He pulls a chair out and I add another plate and silverware.

After Max says grace, I study both men's faces since they were being quiet. Putting my fork down, I cross my arms. "All right give. What's going on?"

Noah looks at me than at Max. "We might as well tell her, she'll either hound us to death or find out on her own."

Max gives me a scowl, which I ignore then he sighs. "It seems there is someone asking around about the mansion and who owns it now. They also have been to the courthouse to look up the records on the mansion and from the description being given, it's making me a little uncomfortable."

I wait for him to continue. "Would you care to elaborate on that?"

"Tall, on the slender side, probably mid to late thirties, dressed in worn jeans, t-shirt and a leather jacket. They also have a scar over their left eyebrow that runs down the side of their face. I also heard that he talked with a slight slur." Noah continues to eat after giving that bit of information.

Picking my fork back up, "So why not tell me? Probably someone that thought it was still for sale." I wasn't about to let on that it was strange that just before we were getting ready to open, someone was asking about the mansion.

Max looks at me before turning his attention to Noah. "Thanks for telling us. But maybe Maggie's right, could just be someone that thought it was still for sale." His attention turns back to me with a fork waving in my direction. "But you be careful. We don't know what this man really could be after and until I find out or find him and ask him a few questions, I'd like for you to stay home."

Noah snorts at that before looking at Max. "You do know your wife right?"

Max nods. "I do, anyway I can talk you into keeping an eye on her when I'm not around?"

Wiping his mouth, Noah looks at me. "We both know she's going to manage to do what she wants, but I can try." He turns back to Max. "Why not just put a patrol out here, or handcuff her to the stove?"

All three of us were quiet for a moment and then burst out laughing, including me. Once I recover, I point my fork at Max. "Try that and see where you sleep for a year."

Wiping his eyes Max says. "Okay, just promise to be careful and if anyone comes up here you don't know, do not answer the door. Call me or Noah."

I relinquish a little. "Fine. But we will have people here I don't know in a couple of days."

"That's right. New Years is two days away and then we're officially a business." Shaking his head. "Time do fly." He looks at Noah. "Thanks for the information and if you don't mind, watch her when you can."

Noah nods. "So you want to go up the mountain and you asked if there were any other houses up there. I don't ever remember seeing any and I've never heard of anyone living up there but there is a place where the remains of a foundation are, you want to see that?"

"Yes. From what I've found out there should have been another residence close to the mansion years ago. I don't think it's your cabin from the description."

Picking his plate up and walking to the sink. "What time?"

"Around 10 am?"

"I'll pick you up. Thanks for dinner, it was delicious." Turning to Max. "And I'll try to keep her out of mischief."

After Noah leaves, Max turns to me. "So anything for dessert?"

I look at my husband before shaking my head. "I don't understand how you can eat all of that food and then want dessert. There's blueberry pie." Grabbing the plates, I take them to the sink before bringing the pie to the table with a clean plate and knife. "Here you go."

As I clean the kitchen, I think about what Max and Noah had said, that a strange man was asking questions around town. Why not just come here if he was so curious, unless there was another reason for the nosing around. Was he another Carson? Or a relative? Or could he be connected to the Cambridge's? I had a feeling there was more to both couples than just stopping on their way South.

Chapter 11

The next morning after Max leaves for work, I get my laptop out to see if I could find anything else on the Carson's, the history was sketchy, so I try to see if there was a family tree. But the name was so common that thousands came up. I remember how Joy taught me to sneak into the county records, so looking around, for what I don't know since I was by myself, I pull up the website and sneak in.

I feel a little guilty doing it, but it had helped me before. Finding the original Carson's, I read over what I had already found then come across a warrant for a James Carson. The relationship wasn't clear, but at one time they shared the same address. But the warrant was for attempted bank robbery. Well that wasn't good. And it seems that he was never arrested for the crime.

Searching a little more, I find a death certificate for a James Carson, I wonder if it was the same one? Not finding anything else, I close the site and then shut the laptop off just as Noah comes in the back door. "Good morning Noah. I'll be ready in just a minute."

Baby comes and rubs against his leg, bending down he picks her up, "You really do like it here don't you?" He sits down and holds her and I put a few things up and grab my keys and phone.

"Okay, I'm ready."

Noah puts Baby down, we leave, making sure the door was locked behind me, I walk toward the driveway when Noah clears his throat. Turning to face him, he nods toward the garden where I see a large ATV sitting. Turning back to Noah. "Seriously?"

Noah smiles as he walks toward the monster machine. "Yep, can't drive to where the foundation is, so this will have to do."

As I walk to the ATV. "Well I'm up for a new adventure. Let's do this." Waiting for him to get on before climbing behind him, I notice that the seat was a lot larger than a motorcycle seat, which I was glad for.

Taking the path between our properties instead of the road, he heads for the mountain path and I was thinking this machine was too big for the path, but it fit easily as he starts climbing the steep path.

Taking in the scenery, even though the trees were mostly bare, it was still a beautiful view. Noah slows down as we reach a level area, where no trees were growing.

Stopping the ATV, I climb off and walk over to where there were rocks laid out in somewhat of a square. Walking around the rocks didn't tell me much except that any house that had been here had a fantastic view of the valley.

Noah was studying the layout of the rocks, then bends down and pulls one loose, it crumbles in his hands. Getting up, he wipes his hands off then looks at me. "I don't think this was a house foundation, maybe a barn or shed." Kicking at the rocks, "This is just blocks dug from the ground."

"So no house here. Anywhere else one could have been?"

Noah turns and looks down the mountain into the valley, after a few minutes. "I can only think of one place that would be level enough and that's beside the family cemetery."

I walk over and follow his gaze. "Cemetery? Where?" No one had ever said anything about a family cemetery.

"Come on." Leading the way back to the ATV, we get on and head back down the mountain.

The cemetery where the Cambridge's were buried was behind the mansion, but other than them, there were no other graves. So who was in the family cemetery?

Noah heads for the road this time and once he was heading back down the mountain, he turns off just before reaching his cabin. Pushing our way through the brush until it opens up into a small clearing. Stopping the ATV, we get off and I follow as Noah leads the way to an iron fence that had been overtaken with weeds and vines.

Finding an opening, we walk through and I see several headstones. Tall, ornate headstones. Stopping in front of one, I wipe the dirt off the reveal the name, 'August Cambridge, 1842-1910.' Racking my brain, I don't remember seeing that name in any of the records I had searched. Another stone had the name, 'Florence Wright,' along with several other Wrights. "Who are the Wrights?"

Noah shrugs. "I have no idea."

We walk through the small cemetery to see several stones with Cambridge and several more with Wright, all had passed away before 1920, when the first part of the mansion had been built. Hum.

After looking at the last headstone, I venture
out of the small cemetery and walk around finding
another small clearing and another foundation.
"Noah, come see."

When he reaches me and sees the foundation, he
leans down and tries to pull one loose. "Now these
are river rock, so I think this may have been
another house.

I almost jump up with joy for discovering more
about the Cambridge's before stopping myself. "So
there was another house here. I wonder if this could
have been the parents or grandparents?"

Noah shakes his head a little. "It may be hard
to find out since records weren't kept then, but I
can do a little digging for you."

"Thank you Noah."

We head back to the mansion to see that Max
was home.

Chapter 12

I thank Noah for helping me before heading inside to find Max fixing himself a huge sandwich from the one left over pork chop from the night before. "Think that's enough food?" I stand beside him and shake my head. "I was going to heat that for your supper."

Max smiles before giving me a kiss on the forehead. "Hum, guess you'll have to find something else for dinner." Taking his plate to the table, he sits down then bows his head. When he raises it he asks. "Find anything today?"

"Yes, we did. The place where Noah thought may have been a house turns out to have been maybe a barn, but he took me to the family cemetery and we found another foundation, this one he's sure was a house. So yes, there were more people living here. Oh and I found out there may have been some Wrights related to the Cambridge's, I'll have to do some more research and we really need to clean that cemetery up. Vines and brush have pretty much taken over."

Max stares at me for a minute. "Leave it to you to find more relations to the Cambridge's." He takes another bite and frowns. "You said Wright?"

I nod.

"There were several families with that name years ago. Most of them passed away and I believe there were a couple of children that moved away, but I don't think they were related, at least I never heard that."

"I can look that up too." Rubbing my hands together. "Oh this is so interesting."

With a smile he says, "Better that than getting involved in a murder."

I almost have a comeback then think of something else. "Anything else on Mrs. Hopkins?" I had called Betty and she was going to get a couple of the ladies to talk to the police.

Nodding, he says, "Yes. A couple of women met with Officer Spence and went through the house. As far as they can tell, nothing seems to be missing."

"Did you find out if she had any relatives?"

"Yes, a nephew. But we can't find anything other than his name and the last place he lived, which was in Richmond. But nothing now. It seems he's disappeared."

Drumming my fingers on the table. "The man that's been asking around about the mansion, think he may be the nephew?"

Dropping the rest of his sandwich, he looks at me with surprise. "Why would you think that?"

Shrugging my shoulders. "A stranger in town, asking questions. He came right after she was killed."

"Exactly. Right after she was killed. Unless he's the killer, he got here awful fast and we haven't released any information on it, so how would he know?"

I think on that for a minute, because if he wasn't the killer, how would he know to come at this time? Getting up to fix myself something to drink, I ponder that for a minute, unless he had come to see his aunt hoping to find that she maybe had some extra cash. Sadly that's what estranged relatives did, stay away until they need something.

Sitting back down as Max takes the last bite of his sandwich, I ask, "Wonder if he was looking for a handout?"

Wiping his mouth, Max looks out the window for a minute before answering me. "That would awful convenient now wouldn't it? But it may be something to look into, because we don't even know this is the nephew, could be just a tourist looking for a fancy place to stay." With a smile he picks his plate up and takes it to the sink. As he was rinsing it off the doorbell rings.

"I'll get it."

"No you won't." Wiping his hands he heads for the front door, when he opens it, there's a tall, slender man and the thing I notice first it the scar. "Can I help you?" Max sounds a little intimidating.

"Hello. My name is Jacob Woods and was looking for some information on the history of this house. I don't mean to be intruding, but I think some of my relatives owned this at one time."

The man was clearly nervous, which made me wonder if what he was saying was true. With Max here, I was all right with inviting him here. "Well we can certainly talk, please come in."

As the man enters the house, Max gives me a look over his head. "Yes, let's talk." If the man had been nervous before, just the way Max had said that would make him nervous.

I lead the way to the kitchen and point to the table. "Please sit down. Can I offer you something to drink?"

Sliding his backpack to the floor, he sits down and clasps his hands together. "No thank you."

Well he had manners, no matter who he was.

Max sits back down in his chair. "Care to tell us your story and why you think you may be related?"

I take my seat again and smile at the man.

"Um… like I said my name is Jacob Woods and my mother was Emma Wright. She was raised here and always talked about what a great town it was. She told me that she really hated leaving town after dad got a job in South Carolina." He stops talking and clears his throat. "I saw an ad about this house for sale and thought about how my mother talked about it, but when I got here found out it had sold."

His voice was cracking, so I get up to fix him a glass of water. Handing it to him, I ask. "Were the Wrights related to the Cambridge's in some way?"

After taking a sip of water, he nods. "Mom's side was related to Mrs. Cambridge, her brother was mom's uncle." Taking another sip. "Do you have any history of the house?"

Max had relaxed a little, "Very little, only what we found when we bought the house. Most is on the Cambridge side."

Jacob nods. "Yeah from mom has told me, I took it that the Cambridge's were a little on the controlling side."

I frown at the words then remember some of the things that I had read about Mr. Cambridge and how he had treated his wife. Of course at the time, most women were more or less subservient to their spouses so it hadn't surprised me. "Let me get the photo album I found." I get up and head for the den and my little corner of history on the house as Max asks how long Jacob was planning on staying.

Chapter 13

Grabbing the album, I return to the kitchen to see both men were having an easy conversation. Laying the album on the table, I push it in Jacob's direction. He stares at the book like it may bite him before reaching for it.

Opening the cover, he studies the first page and reads the small card I had put in with who was in the first photo. We're quiet as he slowly goes through the album, stopping on a page with a couple that I couldn't find the names of. He smiles a little then points to the photo. "This is my grandma and grandpa. I didn't know them well."

"Do you remember their names?" I had a pen and paper ready to take notes.

He nods. "Jacob and Thelma Wright. I was named after him." He flips a few more pages and the smile on his face is replaced with a scowl.

Max notices too. "What's wrong?"

Jacob looks up at Max. "Oh nothing, just trying to remember names, but you have them here on these cards." He goes through the rest of the album and slowly closes the cover. "Thank you. That meant a lot." He pushes the album back to me. "I've taken enough of your time. Maybe we can get together again before I leave town."

Max takes a chance. "Where are you staying?"

Jacob picks his backpack up. "Oh, at the motel." Sliding the straps over his shoulders, "I probably won't be in town much longer. But thank you." He holds his hand out for Max to shake, nods at me and turns toward the door.

I stay in the kitchen while Max escorts him out. When he comes back into the kitchen, he sits down and looks at me. "Believe him?"

Looking at Max before shaking my head, "Not everything. I do think that was a picture of his grandparents by the look on his face, but not much else. And what motel is he staying at? There aren't any here except for the one that's closed next to the old gambling casino."

"Exactly. When you went to get the album, he was looking around pretty hard." Leaning toward me, he takes my hand. "I do not want you to be alone with this man. He may be on the up and up, but right now I just want to be careful." He squeezes my hand. "Promise?"

I had the same feeling so it wasn't hard to promise. "I promise. He made me just a little uncomfortable there at the end anyway." Pulling the album to me, I flip until I get to where I thought the picture made him angry. It was a picture of Mr. Cambridge standing in front of the mansion holding the keys in his hand. Tapping the photo. "Why would this picture make him angry?"

Max turns the album toward him and studies it. "I don't know. Unless he's just mad at Cambridge."

"But why? He didn't know him. Maybe there's some bad blood between the Wright's and the Cambridge's. Something to keep in mind."

Shutting the album, he slides it to me. "I still don't want you around him alone and if he comes back and I'm not here, call Noah or the station and don't let him in." Getting up. "I need to get back to the office and see if they have anything else on Mrs. Hopkins."

I nod before asking. "And what do you want for dinner?"

Rubbing his stomach, "We may be skipping dinner, so go ahead and have what you want." Kissing me on the cheek. "And remember, do not let him in if he comes back."

Giving him a mock salute, "Yes sir. I won't sir."

"Smarty-pants." Shaking his head, he leaves the house by the back door then turns and motions for me to lock it.

Getting up, I do as he asks before picking the album up again. Opening it to the picture that Jacob scowled at, I study it, but it just seems to be an innocent picture of a man glad to have possession of the keys to the mansion. Maybe I need to do some more research on the mansion. Taking the album back to my little corner in the den, I start to put it back on the shelf, but something told me to put it in a drawer for now, so I carry it across the room and tuck it under some tablecloths I had in the armoire, patting the cloth before closing the drawer.

Chapter 14

Leaving the den, I return to the kitchen to finish cleaning from lunch and then call Mary Ann. Not getting an answer, I leave a message to come by when she had a chance to make a couple of changes on the inn's reservation page.

Well now, the house was clean, we were ready for our guests and there was plenty of food in the house. So what now?

Pulling my laptop out, I start doing some research on the Wrights, there were so many in the cemetery and now that I knew they were acquainted with the Cambridge's, I needed to know more.

Getting so wrapped up in the history of River Oaks and the people, I didn't notice that someone was at the front door until I hear a yell. Going to the door, I almost open it before remembering what Max had said, so I look out the peephole to see Mary Ann.

Opening the door. "Sorry I was on the computer."

"I was getting ready to call Max. So how are you?" Mary Ann tucks her phone back in her bag.

"We're fine. I'd like some changes on the website though." We walk to the small desk I had in the alcove with the computer. "One of the guests that's coming this weekend smokes, so I would like for you to state that no smoking is allowed. And can you walk me through the reservation page again. I think I put a guest in wrong."

Mary Ann smiles as she makes herself comfortable at the computer. "No problem, let me get

that no smoking on first and we'll go from there."
As she types, she asks. "So I heard about Mrs.
Hopkins and the rumor is she was killed by someone
she knows."

Shaking my head as I watch Mary Ann type.
"Speculation. But there was a mark on her neck they
think was caused by a needle, but nothing is for
sure yet." I wonder if Elsie had anything to do with
that?

Finishing updating the website, Mary Ann pulls
up the reservation page and walks me through the
process again, which I basically had right except
for types of payment. "Strange all the reservations
are for people named Carson."

"Yes I know and I'm a little concerned. I
found that there were Carson's acquainted with the
original Cambridge's. I'm hoping it's just a
coincidence."

After we finish, I fix a pot of tea and we sit
at the kitchen table and talk. Filling her in on our
visit from Jacob Woods and his reaction to the
picture in the album.

"Sounds like he has an issue with the
Cambridge's, but since there aren't any left, why is
he here?" Mary Ann frowns. "I think I agree with Max
on not being alone with him."

Twirling my cup around. "I agree. It's just I
think there's more than just an issue with past
relatives. I mean why come when you know there
probably aren't any relations left and from little
bit he said and what Max has told me, there aren't
any Wrights left either. So why come at all?"

Mary Ann sits for a moment before saying, "Is there any possibility he could be trying to get the mansion as an inheritance?"

Shaking my head, "No, the house was free and clear when we bought it. Noah even went over everything before we signed the final papers. And there have been other owners besides us through the years."

"We also know there wasn't a treasure buried like people believed. Wait…maybe that's it, he doesn't know the treasure was the roses and thinks that it's still on the property somewhere."

I sit up straight. "You may be on to something there." I think on that for a minute, "The Carson's, what if they're coming for the same thing?" A little wave of apprehension crawls up my spine. "What if they all are trying to find the treasure and will tear the house apart and the garden?" Standing up, "Maybe having an inn wasn't such a good idea."

Mary Ann grabs my hand and pulls me back down. "Calm down. We don't know anything yet. But it may be a good idea if you and Max fill a couple of other rooms with officers."

My eyes widen at her statement and then I think on it for a minute. "You know that may be a good idea. We don't know these people, then this Jacob Woods comes around asking questions and who knows who killed Mrs. Hopkins. Yes, you're right. I'll talk to Max tonight."

Mary Ann smiles then gets up. "I have to go meet with a tenant interested in renting the house on Elm Street, so I'll talk to you later and let me know if there's anything else I can do."

Giving her a hug as she leaves, I make sure the dead bolt is thrown before going back to my laptop. Except big brown eyes glaring at me from the kitchen window stops me. "Blackie! Hey boy." I grab a handful of carrots before going out the back door to see my horse friend.

The first thing Blackie does is nudge me with his massive head, as I rub his nose, I hold a carrot out in my hand, with a little neigh he gobbles it before nudging my hand for another one. "You're such a sweet boy. Did you come over here by yourself?"

"No, he didn't"

I look around Blackie to see Noah crossing the patio. "Hello Noah, what brings you two boys out?"

"Just checking on things. Any visitors?"

Nodding my head, I fill him in our visit from Jacob Woods then add. "I feel like he's here for more than just reminiscing. We have three rooms booked for people by the name of Carson." Noah knew the history of the mansion as well as I did if not better.

Noah eyes widen just a bit. "Now that is strange."

"Mary Ann suggested I get Max to have a couple of officers stay here at the same time. I think it may be a good idea until we find out if they're really here just passing through or think there really is a treasure still here."

Noah snorts. "Ah the power of folk tales. Maybe we should let them know what the treasure really was. Maybe put a little story sheet or frame a picture of the rose with the legend behind it."

I drop my hands from rubbing Blackie's nose. "What a good idea!" Getting a push in the middle of my back from a huge horse head, I turn back to rub his side.

"Thanks. I can make one and have it here before the first guest checks in." Noah reaches for Blackie's halter.

"Thanks Noah, I'd appreciate that." Giving Blackie another rub on his nose. "You be a good boy."

Leading Blackie away, they walk through the hedges back to his cabin just as Max pulls up in front of the garage. I wait until he joins me. "Hi chief. How was your day?"

"Better now. Got any tea made?"

"Hot or cold?"

"Cold please."

We go inside the house with Max shutting and locking the door behind us. He sits down at the table and I study his face before fixing his glass of tea and notice a little tension.

Chapter 15

Setting the glass in front of him before I sit down and look at him. "Did something happen today?"

He looks at me like he had to tell me something bad. "The techs went over Mrs. Hopkins' house today."

I wait for him to finish, knowing it wasn't going to be good news. "And?"

"The only fingerprints they found on the door were Elsie's."

Letting what he just said sink in before I pull my cell out, but Max puts his hand over mine. "I need to talk to her."

"She's at the station. We have her in interrogation until the rest of the report comes in." Leaning toward me and taking my hands. "I know you want to be there, but since she's such a good friend, I don't know if that's a good idea."

Knowing he was just keeping my best interest at heart, but it still made me a little angry. "She's a friend, she may tell me things that she won't tell you. Ever think of that?"

"Yes I did. I also thought of the fact that if she was in that house anytime before Mrs. Hopkins died, she's s suspect. I can't have you influencing what she says in any way." He drops his eyes to my hands as he squeezes them. "I don't like to see you angry, but I also have a job to do. Once we talk to her and she can confirm what time she was in the house, then I'll let you see her." He looks up at me. "Deal?"

Even though I knew he was right, I still felt as if I was letting Elsie down and there was no question that she didn't so this, even though she and Mrs. Hopkins had words every now and then, but just about everyone in town did. I look in Max's eyes and could see the worry and concern there. "Deal." Conjuring up a small smile for him. "But you know in your heart she didn't so this, so I'll wait until you tell me when I can go see her."

Max smiles. "Thank you." Letting go of my hands, he drinks the rest of his tea. "I have to go back to the station and hoping that if they found anything else it will point to someone else." Standing he leans down and kisses the top of my head. "And I'm sorry."

Nodding at what he said, he leaves, shutting the door softly behind him. I sit for a while and think about Elsie, there was just no way she could have done anything, I know she got aggravated with Mrs. Hopkins and lost her temper with her, but so had I and several other people in town. And when was the last time she had gone over there for her fingerprints to be on the door. Hum, I wonder if they were on the door itself or the doorknob? Picking my cell out, I call Max. "Sorry to bother you, but the fingerprints, where they on the door or the doorknob? You know that Elsie always puts her hands on the door to close it and not the knob."

"That is a good question. Let me find out and I'll let you know."

Hanging up, I knew there was no chance of me doing anything until I hear back from Max, so I pick up my Bible and my tea and go onto the patio. Maybe a little sunshine and conversation with God will help.

Settling on a chaise, I close my eyes and try to focus but my mind was wandering, so I open my Bible and let it fall open. The first verse I see is Psalm 103:6, the Lord executes righteousness and justice for all who are oppressed. A peace fills me and I know that Elsie will be all right. Closing my Bible, I think on the verse for a few minutes and then close my eyes, letting peace fall over me.

A loud noise jerks me awake, I sit up straight and look around. What was that noise? Then I see Noah hammering in stakes for the fence that we were putting around a small area for a vegetable garden. Leaning back, I let my heart calm down as I watch Noah then I hear footsteps. Max comes around the corner and when he sees me, he smiles. Oh he had good news, I hope.

Sitting down in the chaise beside me and turning his head toward me. "Well after talking to Elsie and finding out she had been at Mrs. Hopkins last week at the prayer meeting, she also said her prints should be in the bathroom and on the desk in the den, she said she snuck in there and looked around a little."

I laugh. "Leave it to Elsie to be snooping. So she isn't a person of interest any longer?"

"Well, she is, but we're not holding her now. The door knob was wiped clean, so that tells us if it had been Elsie she would have wiped the door too. No, it's someone else."

Before I could answer, Elsie herself storms around the side of the house. When she sees Max sitting there, her face turns red. "Max I should be mad at you even though I know you're just doing your job, but you know me and that's what hurts."

Getting up, Max wraps and arm around Elsie's shoulders. "I never believed you did, but I had to bring you in and question you, you know that. As much as you've been around Margaret you know that."

Elsie tries to pout a little more, but it wasn't working because a smile breaks out. Patting Max on the chest. "I know. It was kind of exciting to be put in that room and questioned though." She sits down in front of me. "Margaret that was so exciting, oh I was scared at first because I thought that maybe me snooping around her house had gotten me in trouble, you know, invading her privacy and all that, but when they knocked on my door and told me I needed to come in for questioning, oh that was exciting!"

You couldn't help but laugh at the woman and I did. "Leave it to you. I wish I could have watched them question you though." I look over at Max. "Who did question her?"

His face turns a little pink. "I did and Spence was with me."

Elsie claps her hands. "Oh he's so good looking, truth be told I didn't mind him at all, it was fun to look at him."

I glance over at Max to see him trying to hold a laugh in but couldn't and he busts out a loud snort as he tries to hold it.

Leaning forward, I look at Elsie in the eye. "Care to tell us exactly why you were snooping when you were there?"

Casting her eyes down. "Well you know how private she is and always fussing at everyone, I just thought there may be something there that might

give me a clue on why, but the only thing I found
that was interesting was a letter from her nephew
and that wasn't very much."

     Max looks at Elsie. "I shouldn't ask you this,
but what was in the letter?" The nephew had held
Max's interest when he found out he was the only
relative.

     "Just that he was sorry he hadn't kept in
touch and wanted to know if he should come and visit
so they could get to know each other before he heads
oversea for his new job." Elsie turns back to me. "I
saw her bank statement too, that woman was loaded!"

     "Elsie!"

Chapter 16

After admonishing Elsie for being so nosy, she left and we went inside to see what to have for dinner. As I was surveying the contents in the refrigerator, Max reminds me. "Hey New Year's Eve is tomorrow. So what are we going to do?"

"Seriously? Tomorrow? That means our first guests will be here in two days!" I was starting to wonder if this inn idea was a good one. "Oh Mary Ann made the suggestion to have a couple of undercover officers stay here until we find out what Jacob wants and if these people are related to the Carson's that were friends with the Cambridge's."

Max frowns for a minute before saying. "That may be a good idea. Let me toss the idea to a couple of the guys and see if I get any volunteers."

Putting down the head of lettuce I was holding. "Max, I don't have a good feeling about this. I know I may be reading more in this, but something just doesn't sit right with three couples with the name Carson checking in and then someone that claims to be a relative of original…"

Max holds his hand up. "You don't have to explain, I understand and I agree. That's one reason I'm agreeing to some men staying here. Have you discussed this with Noah?"

"Not in detail, but he's thinking they're here for the treasure so he's making some signs that explain what the treasure really is. So if that's what they're here for, they'll realize it was all a tale."

"Now that is a good idea. If I were you, I'd put some of the things we found that gives the

Cambridge history up. We don't want just everyone
going through that desk. Might think of moving all
the old books to our room for the time being."

Setting two plates on the table with turkey
sandwiches and chips. "You said you wouldn't be too
hungry, is this all right?"

Smiling, he nods. "Perfect." Taking my hand,
he says a prayer asking for guidance and thanking
Him for our blessings. When he finished he asks,
"Now tomorrow night. I was thinking of grilling some
steaks, eating on the patio then going up the hill
in the backyard and watch the fireworks."

I smile at my husband. "That would be nice.
And I'm looking forward to it just being us."

A short knock on the back door tells me Noah
was here, before I could get up, he walks into the
room carrying a large square piece of wood.

"Hey. I finished that plaque I was talking
about." He props the piece of wood on the table, on
it was a beautiful picture of the Treasure Rose and
in delicate script, he had written out the story.

"Noah that is beautiful." Smiling at him, I
see a little blush creep up his cheek.

Max wipes his mouth. "Noah I must agree that
is beautiful and thoughtful. I think there's a frame
that might fit that in the attic. We'll check it out
in a few minutes."

"Do you want anything to eat? I can make
another sandwich."

Shaking his head. "No thanks, I'm fine."
Pulling a chair out, he sits down, placing the

placard beside the table. "I did a little research. I couldn't find anyone by the name of Jacob Woods that any connects to the Wrights that were here."

A scowl crosses Max's face. "I had a feeling. Can you see if there is any connection to Mrs. Hopkins? Her first name is Gladys and I think her maiden name was Caulder."

Noah nods. "Already have. Nothing there either. No relations anywhere that I could find. Seems like neither one was from a very large family and they never had any children, she didn't have any siblings and he had a brother, but what I found was that he passed away in prison with no family."

"Oh this gets more and more stressful." I look at Max. "Mind if I just call these people and tell them we're cancelling their reservations and we'll rethink this inn idea."

Taking my hand. "I was never a great fan of the idea anyway. But let's see what happens with these couples and go from there. It's not as if we really need the money."

Chapter 17

As Max and Noah go into the attic to find a frame for the placard, I head back to the computer and look up the reservations again, halfway tempted to cancel them all. There wasn't anything new to see, so I close the page and look at the additions Mary Ann had put on the website. At the bottom she had boldly stated no smoking on premises, that made me smile. She had some really good photos of the inn and the rooms on the site, so good it actually made me want to stay there.

Scrolling through the pictures, I feel a little tug on my pants leg, looking down to see Baby sitting there. "What's wrong little girl?" Picking her up, she cuddles against my chest and snuggles in, giving me a little purr. Rubbing her head, "You miss Tom don't you?" Getting another purr. "I'm sorry girl, hopefully he'll be home soon."

Looking at the clock, I realize that we're supposed to meet the interim pastor in an hour. Shutting the computer down and hugging Baby a few more minutes before I set her down. "Sorry girl, I have to go."

In the kitchen, I feed the cats and put some fresh water in their bowls before going into the bathroom to make sure I looked presentable enough to meet the pastor. Back in the kitchen I find Max and Noah with a large ornate frame and an easel.

"There was an easel in the attic?"

"You wouldn't believe some of the things that are up there. We'll need to straighten it out eventually." He turns the frame toward me and I smile. "Need to fix this one corner." He points to a large chip in the frame then sets the frame on the easel.

"Noah, I'll say it again. It's beautiful. And if that doesn't clear up the legend of the treasure, I don't know what will." Looking at the clock. "Oh, I'm going to be late." Giving Max a kiss goodbye, I grab my keys and head to my car.

Pulling into the church lot to see that it seems like I was the last one to arrive. Entering the church, I walk down the hall to the room where we normally meet. Walking in the room to a full house and a very nice looking young man at the head of the table.

Ross Gillen was chatting with Betty as I sit down. I nod at the others and wait until Betty starts the meeting. When she turns her head to see we were ready, she stands. "Good evening. I'd like to introduce Pastor Ross Gillen. I'm going to let him tell you about himself and you can ask any questions you like." Sitting back down, she smiles and nods at the pastor.

Standing, he introduces himself and then starts telling us his credentials, which were impressive. With a pleasant smile, he says, "Anyone have any questions?"

"Can you tell us about your family?" Mrs. Johnson was smiling as she asked the question.

"It would be my pleasure." He tells us about his wife and three daughters, their interests and what they would like to do in the church. The whole time he was talking there was a look of happiness and love on his face. I could tell he was a good family man.

A few more questions were asked on his plans and if there would be anything that he would change. His reply to all was that he would work with us in any capacity and that until he saw what activities and groups we had, he wouldn't request any changes.

Betty smiles and stands up. "I think we have everything we need. Thank you pastor for meeting with us and we're having refreshments in the fellowship hall to let the members get to know you." With a nod to us, "Meeting adjourned, let's all go to the fellowship hall. Mrs. Dunfree has made us her famous chocolate cake." That got people moving, with a couple lagging behind to talk.

Entering the fellowship hall to the aroma of coffee, I bypass that table and head for the sweets. Mrs. Dunfree's chocolate cake was the absolutely best ever and of course she wouldn't share her recipe. Grabbing a slice, I head for a table and joined a few minutes later by Betty and the pastor.

Wiping my hand before offering it to the pastor. "It's really nice to meet you." With I hope a genuine smile.

Smiling back at me, I notice his dimples and really how young he appeared. "It's my pleasure. I must say this church is quite impressive. The rocks, being beside the river and the sanctuary is breathtaking. It's going to be a privilege to preach until Tom gets better." He takes a bite of the cake and I smile when his eyes widen.

"Really good isn't it?" I smile as he nods.

"Oh my, it is." Laying his fork down, "My wife is going to want the recipe."

"Good luck with that. Mrs. Dunfree won't share her recipe."

I watch the interaction between Ross and Betty and think how nice he is and I actually had a good feeling about him. I think he's going to be a good fit to our church.

"Can you tell me what groups you have?" His gaze was direct and intent, which I liked.

Betty and I filled him in on all the groups that were currently active, he was impressed with the women's' groups, the youth projects and the men's group that helped with handyman chores for the shut-ins and elderly. He seemed excited that we have something for just about everyone in the church.

"I'm excited to be here to help. Have either of you talked with Pastor Tom recently?"

"He was doing better the other day. The doctor seems to think once all of the medication is out of his system he should be fine. And he was happy to hear that you would be in the pulpit."

With a slight blush and a nod. "Thank you, I will do my best to help in every way I can." He turns to me. "I must ask. I've heard that you are somewhat of a sleuth."

Now it was my turn to blush. "Um, well…"

Betty slaps her hand on top of mine. "Yes she is. She gets involved in any crime that happens in town, although the last time she was hurt pretty bad." She looks at me. "Has Max put a stop to you getting involved?"

Shaking my head, "No, he just said to be careful." I turn to Ross. "I was knocked on the back of my head that took a little time to heal. But…" I raise a finger. "We did apprehend the guys that were pushing bad medication on a large part of town."

"This sounds interesting. Maybe once I'm settled in we can talk and you can tell me some of your adventures."

"I'll be glad too." I glance at my watch. "Oh goodness, I need to go." Turning to Ross, I hold my hand out. "It was a pleasure and I'm looking forward to hearing you preach Sunday."

Getting a good-bye from both, I leave the church and head back home to make one last inspection of the house, because tomorrow we will busy with New Year's Eve plans.

Chapter 18

As I drive up the mountain, I think about Pastor Ross and what a good fit he appears to be. Although he was much younger than pastor's we've had in the past, his enthusiasm was a little contagious. I was looking forward to his sermon Sunday and hopefully the rest of the congregation would be too.

Pulling into the garage, I sit for a minute as my mind returns to the Carson's and whether they were really here on a stop in their travels or had motives. Sighing, I grab my purse and get out. Walking to the fishpond, I sit on the edge and watch the little critters swimming. Grabbing a handful of pellets, I toss them in the water and watch as they snatch a mouthful and swim away, coming back for more. Smiling as they eat and swim, I think how relaxing it must be, because it sure was just to watch them.

A few minutes later, I hear the back door shut and then Max sits down beside me. "How was the meeting?"

Leaning back against my husband, "It was good, everyone seems to like him and he's so energetic." I laugh, "Ed didn't even have any questions for him."

"Well if Ed was quiet, I'm impressed. He must be a really good pastor."

I nod as I let my fingers dangle in the water, feeling a little nibble every now and then. "Any news on Mrs. Hopkins?" I could feel Max stiffen a little so I sit up and turn to look at him. "What is it?"

"The county DA wants to question Elsie again even though I've told him that she has an alibi and can explain her prints being there, but he's adamant that she's the only suspect, even though we found dozens of other prints."

"You do realize that he doesn't like Elsie since she blasted him in public about his lack of common sense. He might be after her for payback." No one really liked the DA, mainly because he thought he was the only one with any intelligence and was the only lawyer qualified to be a DA.

"I know. He wants to have a meeting with her tomorrow. I think it may be a good idea if you're in close proximity, just in case."

Propping my head in one hand, "I will. Although you know there's no stopping her once she gets something in her head and if she thinks he's pointing to her for payback…well…it won't be good."

"And that's why I want you there, you seem to be able to calm her down. The ME also was able to pinpoint that she died between 5:30 and 7 pm. So it was right after your meeting. From the evidence, she walked in the door and the person was right behind her or waiting in the house, but there isn't any sign of a break-in. They're also thinking whoever it was came through the front door because at the back door they would have left footprint in the mud at the door. So, that's where we're at right now."

"And she had all her jewelry on, her rings, watch and the necklace she always wore."

"Yes, her wallet and checkbook were in her purse, so robbery is out." Max stands and stretches. "I think something sweet would be good about now."

Pulling me to my feet, we head inside the house where he goes immediately to the freezer while

I take care of the three cats that were meowing for
food. After filling their bowls, I make sure the
back door was locked then put up my purse before
taking my shoes off and heading into the den to join
Max on the couch. Just as I was getting ready to sit
down, I hear my cell phone chirp, so I go back into
the kitchen to get my phone. It was a text from Noah
that he wanted to talk to both of us. Texting back
to come on up, I rejoin Max in the den. "Noah is on
his way up, says he needs to talk to both of us."

Hearing a light tap on the back door, I go to
let Noah in. When he enters he gives me a smile.
"Hey Maggie." Holding some papers up, "I think I've
found something."

"Come on, we're in the den. Do want anything,
water, ice cream?"

"No thanks, I'm fine." He heads to the den as
I get a bottle of water from the fridge then join
them.

Sitting down beside Max as Noah takes the
chair across from us and from the look on his face,
it wasn't good.

"Okay, I did some checking into Mrs. Hopkins
first. There is a relative left and no matter where
I go, it comes back the same. His name is Jacob
Woods and he's not related to the Wrights, from what
records I could get into to, it looks like his
mother was a Joan Hopkins who was Nancy Hopkins
daughter. It appears she left him at social services
saying she couldn't take care of him. The Woods name
is from the father who relinquished guardianship
also. Now where he got the Wrights name is anyone's
guess but it seems there was a dispute many years
ago with the father of Nancy Hopkins' husband and

the Wrights over land." He points to the ground. "This land. So my guess is he's going to try to get the land from you, but you yourself know we did an intense record search on this property so there's no way he can claim any of." He flips through the papers he was holding. "Now the Carson's. The most I could find was that the Carson's that lived in this area had two sons, who both had between them three sons. So those three sons could be the ones that are coming. Their names were so common, that without more information like a social security number, I couldn't find which ones were the actual relations." He lays the papers on the coffee table, then leans back in the chair.

I glance over at Max who was frowning. "I know this is wrong, but I'm thinking that Jacob Woods killed Mrs. Hopkins." He pulls his cell out. "I'm going to have the guys keep an eye out for him since we don't know where he's staying."

Noah holds a hand up. "Been back to Mrs. Hopkins house since you finished the search?"

Max pales. "No we haven't." Tapping his cell phone, he turns to me. "Be back later."

Chapter 19

After the back door shuts, I look at Noah and raise an eyebrow. He gives me a head shake. "Why do I know this isn't going to be good?" Standing he sighs. "Let's go. I'll drive."

Grabbing my purse as we leave the mansion, we walk to his property next door and get into his car. As we go down the mountain, he looks at me. "You sure about this?"

"Yes. First I want to know if he's there and second I want to know if he's the one that killed Mrs. Hopkins. I think he has enough of a violent temper to mouth off to the officers if they try to arrest him."

Nodding at me as he takes a sharp curve. "Ah you want to see a confession or a confrontation."

"Maybe, or justice. I mean what did Mrs. Hopkins have to do with something he's dredging up from the past? Nothing. She didn't deserve that." Just thinking about it was making me a little angry.

"If he did it. Let's not jump to conclusions just yet." He slows down as he reaches the street that Mrs. Hopkins had lived on.

The street was lit up with the lights from several cruisers. I even see a state trooper's car. This was much bigger than Max and a couple of officers checking the house out. Noah parks as close as he can, but we couldn't see anything. I notice the Johnson's were standing on their front porch, watching the activity. "Let's go see if the Johnson's will let us join them." I nod toward their house.

"You go ahead. I'll stay here."

Walking past the roadblock, I nod at a couple of officers who were making sure no one tried to drive through then reach the house. "Hello Mark, Debra. Care if watch what's going on with you?"

"Come on up Margaret. Can you tell us what's going on?"

Leaning against the porch railing. "They believe someone is camping out in Mrs. Hopkins house and they have suspicions he may be involved with her demise."

Debra claps a hand to her chest. "Oh my, that's terrible!"

"Have you seen any lights on or anyone over there?"

Mark frowns. "I didn't think anything of it, but I did see a young man walking around the house a couple of days ago…let's see, it must have been well, the day after."

Turning to him, I ask, "Can you describe him?"

Shrugging his shoulders, "I really didn't pay much attention, guess I should have with what happened, but let's see, he was slim, I remember that and had a backpack, well that's about all I remember."

Turning my attention back to the house, where I could see the front door open, two uniformed officers on the porch talking, then Max walks out of the house carrying the backpack. And I was sure it was the same one, he hands it to one of his officers then notices me. I wave and get a glare in return.

Ignoring him, I study the house, it was an older two story, not quite a Victorian, but it was around sixty years old. The front porch reached across the whole front of the house, there were two large windows on the first floor. A roof covered the porch and the second floor had two smaller windows. The drapes were drawn at every window. Above the second floor was the attic dormer. The house was painted a soft yellow with black shutters and roof, trimmed in white. Mrs. Hopkins had taken good care of the house and it looked almost new.

Watching as a couple more officers come back out, shaking their heads at Max before stopping to talk to him. Two more state troopers come from the side of the house, one was carrying a large plastic bag.

There really wasn't much going on, so I decide that I would leave but a movement caught my eye. Looking back to the dormer, I see the curtain move. Max was heading this way, probably to fuss at me, but I yell out and point to the dormer. "Max, the attic!"

He turns to follow where I was pointing, then turns and heads back in the house, yelling at a couple of men to follow him.

The Johnson's get up from their chairs and stand beside me as we hear yelling and then the window breaks as a body jumps out landing hard on the porch roof before rolling off and hitting the ground.

Immediately several officers surround him and I see one pulling his radio out. Max joins the men, kneeling beside the body and touching his neck. I was sure it was Jacob Woods and when Max looks up at me and nods, I knew it was.

"Oh my goodness!" Debra puts her hand over her mouth as Mark wraps his arms around her.

"If he survived that, it'll be a miracle." He pats his wife's arm softly before leading her back inside the house.

"Thank you for letting me impose on you." Mark nods as he pulls the screen door shut behind him and I leave the porch and head back to where Noah was parked.

Finding him leaning against the front of his car. When he sees me he shakes his head. "That was wicked. I'd be amazed if he survives that fall."

Turning back to the scene to see that an EMT had arrived and they were loading Jacob onto a gurney. Noah straightens up. "Want to stay?"

Shaking my head. "No I think that was enough. I'll wait until Max gets home."

Chapter 20

Back at the house, I sit on the patio and close my eyes before saying a prayer for Jacob Woods. Opening my eyes, I shake my head, with the way the man landed on the roof and then the ground, it would be a miracle if he wasn't severely injured.

Which reminded me that I haven't seen Tom for a couple of days. Going back into the house, I find the cats in their usual place where the sun is shining at the window seat in the kitchen. Sitting down with them, I take a few minutes to rub each cat before picking Baby up and cuddling her under my chin. "I'm sorry you have to be stuck here with us. But I'm sure Tom will be home soon." Setting the cat down, I find my phone and call Doc to check on Tom.

"Hello Maggie. I was going to call you in a bit. We're moving Tom to a facility in Richmond for a few weeks. He's just not doing as well as I hoped here."

"Oh I'm sorry to hear that, he seemed to be doing a little better the other day and I was hoping that by now he'd be well on his way to recovery."

There was a pause before Doc said, "I'm sorry Maggie, but in my opinion, I really don't think Tom is going to be getting much better. The facility has a therapist on the floor all the time and they specialize in cognitive recovery. He'll be transported tomorrow morning if you want to say goodbye, I'd do it today."

I take a deep breath, "Thanks Doc and I'm on my way."

Picking my purse up, I call Max as I head to the garage, but it goes to voice mail, so I knew

that he was busy. Leaving a message, I get in my car
and head to the hospital to see Tom.

Parking at the side of the hospital, I
recognize Max's truck, so he must be here with Jacob
Woods. Entering the hospital, I go straight to the
elevators and Tom's room. When I enter, I find Tom
standing in front of the window, his hands clasped
behind his back and mumbling. Taking a step closer,
I could hear what he was saying and it appears he
was giving a sermon.

Sitting down in the chair beside the bed, I
wait until Tom turns around before saying anything.
But in the meantime, the sermon he was giving was
one I had heard before on temptation. When he
finishes, he claps his hands together then turns
around. When he sees me, he frowns for a minute and
then smiles. "Maggie! What a surprise!" He sits on
the edge of the bed and smiles at me.

"Hello Tom, I just wanted to come by and see
how you were doing, but it seems like you're doing
fine." I smile as I tell my little fib.

He looks back at me and the look changed from
being happy to see me, to confusion. "Who are you?"

Oh my. "Tom, it's me Maggie." I get up and
step closer to him.

He studies my face for a few minutes, then the
smile returns. "Hi Maggie, how are you?"

He was much worse than he was a couple of days
ago. I pray the place in Richmond could help him. I
start to say something then notice that his eyes
were blank again. I say a prayer before lightly
touching his hand and leave with tears in my eyes. I
had been hoping that Doc had been just a little

wrong, but Tom was worse than he was before and I
have a feeling it didn't have anything to do with
taking the wrong medication.

Sitting in my car, crying, I didn't notice Max
approaching until he opens the passenger door and
gets in.

Seeing my tears, he takes my hand. "Tom?"

I nod. "Oh Max, he's worse than he was. Doc is
going to send him to a facility in Richmond, but I
have a feeling he'll always have memory problems."
Pulling me to his chest, Max wraps his arms around
me, letting me cry. We're both quiet for a few
minutes before I straighten up and wipe my eyes.
Taking a couple of deep breaths, I try a half smile,
"So how's Jacob Woods?"

Max leans back against the door. "Serious but
stable, he'll be here for a while. Both legs are
broken, one arm, several broken ribs, a concussion
and four cracked teeth. They have him so sedated we
couldn't talk to him, but I have a guard on him just
in case, even though he can't move."

"Did he say anything before he jumped out of
the window?"

Max shakes his head. "I believe he thought
we'd leave without finding him, if you hadn't seen
movement upstairs, we probably would have."

"Well he's the one that looked out the window
before you left, so it is his fault. And jumping
from the window just makes him look guilty." Looking
over at Max. "Find anything else in the house?"

He shakes his head. "Not really, you could
tell things had been gone through but we did find a

syringe in the backpack but no insulin and no prints." He taps the dashboard with his fingers. "I think he did it and now we have his prints, we can run those and see what else he's been up too." I nod as my mind goes back to Tom and tears fill my eyes again. Seeing the tears, he takes my hand. "Maggie go home. I'll be home as soon as I can." He raises my chin and gives me a light kiss. "And don't worry about dinner, we'll just raid the fridge."

Giving my husband a smile and nod, "Yes dear. To be honest, I don't want to be alone. I may stop by Elsie's for a little bit." Then a thought occurs. "She's not in jail is she?"

Max laughs as he opens the door. "No dear, there wasn't any evidence to hold her. See you later, if you need me call."

Chapter 21

Pulling into Elsie's driveway, I see her sitting on her front porch reading, even though it was late December, the weather was nice enough to enjoy the porch. She looks up and smiles when she sees me. Putting her book down, she greets me as I step on the porch, "Hey Maggie, what brings you by. And oh, I have so much to tell me. Want some tea or a Pepsi?"

"A tall glass of ice with Pepsi." I sit down in one of the rockers as she goes inside to get my drink. Picking the book up that she was reading, it was a romance novel. Oh really!

Hearing the screen door slam, I smile as she hands me my drink. "Thanks. So how did the questioning go?"

She didn't let me finish before she starts talking. "It wasn't just being questioned by Max, he was just doing his job, it was the District Attorney wanting to question me! Can you imagine that? Oh I wouldn't have answered his questions, but it seems they have another suspect, so they cancelled my meeting with him, just wait until I see him, but I'll make sure it's on the street with witnesses and everything so he can't bring any charges on me for harassing him. Although he needs a good harassment. I don't know what's got into that man, ever since he took office he's been a bullheaded psycho. Anyway what brings you by?"

"I went to see Tom, he's not good. The doctor is going to send him to Richmond to a mental facility, hoping they can work with him, but Elsie, I don't think he'll ever be the Tom we knew."

She pats my knee. "Oh Maggie, I'm sorry. I know you two had a good friendship. My goodness, if you hadn't found him, he may not even be here today." She frowns a little. "Wonder why it affected him and not the others, I mean they were all given the wrong medicine, including me and we didn't have that bad of a reaction."

"I guess it depends on your physical condition and what medicines you were on. I don't know. I'm just sad that he maybe won't ever be the same."

Elsie continues to pat my knee. "It'll be all right, you know that. God will take care of him." She's quiet for a minute, which for Elsie is a long time. "So tell me about this suspect they have now."

That made me laugh, which I needed. "Let me tell you a story." I filled her in on all the Carson's that had made reservations, about Jacob Woods coming to visit and what we found out about him and then what Noah had found. I finished with what had happened today.

"Geez Louise! That's mighty suspicious! Do they have any evidence on him? Is that why they aren't looking at me now, I mean I'm glad they're not, but is that why? And these people that are coming are you sure they're who they say they are? Maybe they're coming to do us all in."

Elsie was rocking the chair so hard I was afraid she was going to tip over. Putting my hand on the arm of her chair, "Easy girl, the only thing we know is that all their names are Carson, it could be a family meeting here or just coincidence, so don't read more into than there is…yet."

"So you have some suspicions too?" A little glimmer was in Elsie's eyes.

Shrugging my shoulders, "A little, but not in a bad way. To be honest I think they're here to find the Cambridge treasure, so Noah made some plaques that explain what the treasure really is and he made a beautiful picture of the rose."

Elsie nods her head. "Good reason. Boy that Noah is handy to have around isn't he? Not bad looking either."

I smack at her arm when she says that. "And you're three decades too old for him."

"Don't hurt to look. Did you meet the new pastor?"

"I did." So I fill her in on our meeting and talking to him afterwards. "I think he's going to fit in nicely. We're going to meet with him again, but I think everyone will like him."

I stay and talk with Elsie for another thirty minutes then look at my watch. "I should go, Max may be home shortly and I want to see if they found anything else out." Getting up. "Thanks for letting me talk, you're a good friend."

Waving her hand at me, "Oh you know better than that. Call me if you need me."

I leave her house and head to the mansion, wondering what will be waiting today.

Chapter 22

Walking into my kitchen to find Max and Noah at the kitchen table with coffee in hand and papers strewn all over the table. Setting my bag down, I john them at the table, standing beside Max. "What are you two doing?"

Max leans back. "Noah brought over everything he found on Jacob Woods and a few interesting things that has surfaced. Join us, you'll want to hear this." Stretching his arms over his head, "Oh, I forgot to tell you, there was a message on the machine when I got home, one of the Carson couples wants to cancel their reservation."

"Huh." I go to the computer in the alcove and replay the message as I pull the reservation list up. It was the last couple that had wanted the end of the week. Interesting. I cancel their reservation and then call the number I have for them. Getting voice mail, I leave a message and thank them. Hanging up, I look at the two couples left, one was due in two days, the other in four days. And here's something I just noticed, both men's name first name was James. Coincidence, no don't think so.

Going back into the kitchen, I fix some snacks before sitting down. "So the last couple that reserved a room cancelled and I just noticed that the other two couples, both of the men are named James."

Max looks at me. "Strange." He hands me a paper. "I've got Spence and Taylor willing to stay here a couple of days and I still think we need to rethink this inn thing if it's going to cause problems."

Looking at the paper he had handed me, I see a picture of Jacob Woods along with a mile long rap sheet. Everything from breaking and entering to altercations with the police and several DUI's. "Hum. If what you found out about his family life is true, this really doesn't surprise me. Except for the DUI's. I didn't get the impression of a heavy drinker unless it was drugs."

"I can check with the police department there. Here's the interesting part." He hands me another report.

Glancing at the form, it appears to be an assault charge and the victim tried to file a lawsuit against Jacob. It appears that a young teenager was given an insulin shot after having an altercation with Jacob, the boy survived, but has some adverse medical problems now. The father is still trying to have Jacob tried, but it seems as if the city attorney where it happened isn't cooperating. "How can the attorney say he isn't going to file charges? It seems there was evidence and here, a witness, so they just let Jacob go?"

"Read the attorney's name."

I did and I drop the paper and stare at Max because the name was James Carson. Getting up, I go to the reservation list and look at where the two couples listed as their home address. Writing down the information, I return to the table and slide the paper toward Max. He looks at the addresses then at Noah. "Can you do a search on these two addresses and see if anything comes back concerning Jacob and whether one of them is the city attorney?"

Noah looks at the addresses and frowns before
digging into the pile of paper. Finding what he was
looking for, he slides the page toward Max.

Max looks at me. "It seems the James Carson
that lives in northern Virginia is the city attorney
that is denying the claim." He taps the table.
"Wonder if Jacob knew they were traveling this way?"

Noah and I look at each other before I give my
opinion, "I think so, but there's a connection with
Mrs. Hopkins some way. We know she was related to a
Wright, so that may have something to do with it,
but why kill her?" I needed to get away from this
problem for a little while. "I need a break." I get
up and head for the den where I pick up my Bible and
sit at the desk, holding it.

Closing my eyes, I concentrate on the Lord and
nothing else for a few minutes before letting my
Bible fall pen to Psalm 119:98, Your commandments
make me wiser than my enemies, For they are ever
mine. I think for a few minutes on the verse,
understanding that the commandments were for me to
follow, so basically mine, along with everyone else
that believes, but I also take it to mean to follow
them to make me wiser in God's Word.

Putting my Bible aside, I think for a little
while, relishing the peace that I had now. I was
going to step back a little and let things fall into
place as they should, even though I'll help some of
it along myself.

Chapter 23

When I go back in the kitchen, I find Max sitting by himself mulling over some of the reports that Noah had left him.

"Want anything to eat?" I open the refrigerator, I wanted something, but not a meal.

Looking over his glasses at me. "Don't you want to read some of this?"

Shutting the door, I turn and look at him. "No. If I find anything out, it'll be because I was supposed to. Me reading all those reports makes me form an opinion, so I'll wait and see what happens and go from there."

Max drops the papers he was holding before taking his glasses off and pulling me into a big bear hug, "I know it's disappointing to wonder if the guests are really here to have a good time or are after something, but it'll be all right. We have someone that will keep us safe no matter what."

Letting a deep breath out, "I know and that's why I'm going to back off a little. Jacob Woods can't tell us anything right now, even if he wanted to. Speculating on why that couple cancelled their reservation isn't right, they may have had a family emergency or something and until I meet the other two couples, I don't want to be imagining what they may do to the inn." I look up into his eyes, "So I'm taking a step back for a day or two. Besides, tomorrow is our first New Year's Eve and I don't want to spoil that with going over old reports."

Max nods before kissing the top of my head. "Good idea. I think I'll just put all this stuff up and we'll go watch some TV."

Since he said we were going to watch TV, I fix some popcorn and a couple of soft drinks, taking it all to the den while he straightens the mess of paper he had on the table.

Once we were settled on the couch, with three cats cuddled around us just waiting for a stray piece of popcorn, we turn on an old movie and let the worries float away. Hearing laughter, I open my eyes with a cat curled in my lap, a large man beside me snoring and the late show on TV.

Jostling Max awake, "Hey, let's go to bed."

With a few grumbles, he lifts the cat off his shoulder and gets up before turning the TV off and then stretching. "Wow that was a nice nap." After a yawn, he smiles, "And Happy New Year Mrs. Gunderson."

Looking at the mantle clock, I realize that he was right, it was officially New Year's Eve, "And Happy New Year to you." Giving him a kiss, he wraps an arm around me as we head for the stairs.

As Max gets ready for bed, I wash my face before pulling the covers back and then let the cats wait for us to get in before finding where they were going to sleep tonight. Giving me a kiss before saying a prayer, Max rolls over and within seconds he was snoring.

Laying there thinking of the possibilities of our guests being up to no good, were slim and then wondering if Jacob will ever tell what was really going on with him and whether he had anything to do with Mrs. Hopkins death, I close my eyes and ask the Lord to clear my mind and let everything that we were speculating on be wrong.

Turning the light off, I roll onto my side with a cat close, a husband even closer and close my eyes, letting sleep take over.

My dreams that night were vivid. Everything from Jacob plunging a syringe into Mrs. Hopkins' neck, to strange people ransacking my house, blaming me for stealing their inheritance, to trying to tear the house apart looking for it.

Startled awake from the last dream, I lay quietly hoping the sound of snoring and the cats grumbling in their sleep would calm my nerves a little, but after a half hour, it wasn't working.

Quietly getting up, I grab my robe and head downstairs for a hot cup of tea thinking it may calm me down.

Leaving only one light on in the kitchen, I sit at the table with my mug and stare out the window into the night. You could see lightning bugs flitting through the night and a little light from the half moon, other than that it was dark, just like my mood.

There was only one thing to clear my mind. Sliding my Bible over, I stick a finger in and open it, I was in Job. I read the story of his doubts and the way God guided him, finally opening his eyes. Closing mine, I let the visions of Job fill my mind and then I pray. Thankful for all my blessings, for my health, for Max, my family, my friends, the church and finally ask forgiveness of my sins.

Keeping my eyes closed, I let my mind run over things that had happened in the last several days, from visiting Tom, to talking to the interim pastor and then Jacob Woods. My eyes open, why did he get so mad at the picture of Mr. Cambridge? Going into the den, I open the drawer and pull out the album, taking it back to the kitchen, I turn the overhead light on before turning to the picture.

First I study the picture, not finding anything odd. It was Mr. Cambridge standing in front of the mansion, the original mansion before any renovations were done to it. He was standing on the front porch, the door was open behind him and he had a huge smile on his face as he holds a large ornate key up. The key to the mansion I thought.

Tapping the table, I had seen that key before, but where? Still studying the picture, there wasn't anything else there. You could see a couple of the treasure rose bushes, part of one of the front windows and the river rock that the house was built out of. Nothing else. Mr. Cambridge was wearing a classic suit with a vest and ascot, typical for that period of time and you could see the chain from his pocket watch, but the key.

I absently flip through the pages again, smiling at some of the pictures and sad at a few of them and the story they told. The last picture was of Mr. Cambridge with his two sons, none of them were smiling, standing stiff as boards and it was taken at the back of the house where the patio was now. Mr. Cambridge had a hand in one pocket and you could see the chain from his pocket watch and the key. If that was the key to the house, why wasn't it in his pocket instead of on a chain he would have to unhook and pull the key from every time he wanted to use it, of course people didn't lock their doors then, but still.

Two hands are placed on my shoulders and squeeze. "Is there a reason you're pouring over the album and not sleeping?"

I look at the clock to see that it was 6 am. "I had a bad dream, well several bad dreams so I came down for some tea and then started looking at the album."

Max sits down, "What kind of dreams?"

Chapter 24

"I dreamed of Jacob, I could see him plunging the syringe in Mrs. Hopkins' neck. The people coming, they were ransacking the house and then tearing it apart. I couldn't sleep anymore, so I came down here and tried to understand why Jacob got so mad at the picture." I tap the album before opening it to the photo. "This one. Remember how mad he appeared when he saw it?"

Max looks at the picture before turning his eyes to me. "It's just a picture of Cambridge in front of the house."

"Yes, but it made Jacob mad." I tap the photo again. "Everything is just a normal picture of a man in front of his house, but the key."

Max studies the key. "It's a key to the house."

Shaking my head. "I don't think so, it's too ornate, it's more a key for a safe or a chest, maybe an armoire, but a house key wouldn't be that large and I've seen the key somewhere before." I slam the album close. "I just can't remember where and I think it's important."

Taking my hand, Max wraps it in his bear paw. "We'll figure it out. Now why don't you try to get a little sleep while I go check on Jacob and see if anything's changed." He kisses my forehead as he gets up and goes upstairs.

A few minutes later, he returns, dressed and ready to start his day while I was still sitting and tapping the album.

"Maggie, go take a nap at least. Turn the TV on and watch one of the crime shows you like, maybe that will clear your mind a little." Giving me another kiss, he leaves, shutting the door quietly behind him.

I look at the clock, it was now 7 am and I wasn't in the least bit sleepy. Going upstairs, I make the bed before getting dressed and shooing the cats to the kitchen where I feed them before they take their place in the window seat.

Every time I pass the album, I think of the key, so I take the album back to the desk and tuck it in a drawer. Out of sight, out of mind, yeah right. Back in the kitchen, I brew a pot of coffee and fix myself a bowl of cereal. Sitting back down at the table, I stare out the window as I mindlessly eat the cereal, then drink the coffee.

Picking the phone up, I call Noah and ask him to come over, there was something I wanted him to see. A few minutes later I hear a light tap on the back door, opening it to let Noah in.

"Anything wrong?" Noah asks as he pours himself some coffee.

"No, but there's something bothering me." I go to get the album again and lay it open in the table. Noah walks over and looks at the photo. "Um, Mr. Cambridge." He looks at the photo again and then me, raising his eyebrows.

"The key. It's too big and ornate for the house, so what does it go to? A safe, a chest? And I know I've seen it before but where?"

Noah sits down and pulls the album closer, then flips through the whole album before getting up. I follow as he goes to the den and directly to the glass case we had set up with mementoes from the Cambridge's. I had small knick knacks, handkerchiefs, a hand fan, just small trinkets, but they filled the whole case.

Noah looks over what I had put in before opening the case and reaching for the small jade case that I had always thought was an antique pill case. Flipping the small latch, he opens the case before handing it to me. Inside was the key.

"I knew I had seen it. But what does it go to?"

Noah takes the key and studies it then tosses it in his hand. "You're right, it doesn't go to a door. But I don't remember seeing any kind of chest that would be large enough for this. We've been through the whole house, no secret doors, no…" He tosses the key again and smiles, "I think I know." I follow as he leads the way to the back door and walks to the fountain where we had the fish.

The fountain was a large oval, made from black marble rock with carvings on the sides. There was a ledge around the whole fountain that you could sit on and gaze into the water. Several pieces of the marble were placed along the top with holes to hold pots of flowers. The bottom had a design etched in of what I always thought may at one time had been mermaids, but over time the design had worn down. The sculpture on the opposite side was of a large fish that water poured from its mouth. We seldom let the water run since we found out it overflowed. Noah had been meaning to fix it, but it was something we had put off.

Sitting on the edge, he kicks his boots off before rolling his jeans up and stepping into the cold water. The fish start swimming around the strange white things that invaded their space. Noah wades to the middle of the fountain and starts sliding his foot back and forth, then he stops. "We haven't fixed the overflow because there isn't a drain built in, but while I was searching for one, I found a keyhole and couldn't figure out what it was." He holds the key up. "Cross your fingers." Leaning down his hands disappear in the water, you could see his arms moving and he utters a few choice words before shaking his head. Standing up, "The key fits, but it won't turn." He looks around the fountain. "If it's anything like the other things we've found, there's a trick somewhere." He looks down at the fish. "We need to drain the fountain but first get the fish out."

Wading back to the side, he climbs out. "I'm going to go get the water trough and get the fish in there before we try to drain the fountain."

I put a hand on his arm, "Noah, can we wait until the guests leave? I really don't want to be looking for something the Cambridge's left with them here because I have a feeling their trip is more than just a stop on their way south."

After rolling his pants legs down, Noah stands and looks at me, "Okay, still think they're up to no good?"

Nodding as we walk back to the patio, "I know I shouldn't jump to conclusions, but first three couples named Carson, then Jacob Woods shows up who's a roundabout relation to the Wrights and I still don't understand the connection to the Cambridge's. Something isn't right with the whole thing and I don't want to be uncovering what could be another treasure while they're here."

"Understood. We'll tackle this mystery after they leave." He starts to hand me the key and then closing his fingers around it. "I think I'll hide this at my place until we're ready."

"Thank you Noah."

With a short nod, he walks toward the hedges and the path to his place.

Chapter 25

Feeling a little better, I head back inside and straighten up from my light breakfast then go back into the den to make sure everything was put away and for good measure, locked the desk and glass case, tucking the keys inside a book I had on the bookcase that had a secret compartment in it, a trick I learned when I found the embezzled money in the church tucked inside several hollowed out books in the library.

Gazing around the room, to make sure everything was in order, I turn the TV on, mostly for the company than to sit and watch anything. Satisfied with the den, I check the arrival time for our first guests, they were to be here by 1 pm on the 2nd, day after tomorrow and I was getting a little nervous. I didn't know if it was the suspicions I had or the fact that total strangers were going to be sleeping down the hall.

I shake off the little zip of anxiety that shimmered down my spine off and went back to the kitchen to find Baby trying to catch a bird that was hovering at the bird feeder we had outside the window. Smiling at her tapping the glass with her paws, I turn to the refrigerator taking the steaks for tonight out and then pull out everything to make a salad.

Singing as I chop the tomatoes, cucumbers and onions, then tearing the lettuce, I finish the salad then cover it and put it back in the refrigerator before turning to the steaks. Rubbing on a few spices and then piercing them with a fork before putting them away, then I wrap some potatoes in foil.

Once I had all the prep work done, I went outside to make sure the grill was ready. When I raise the lid, I jump back at the snarling mouth I see. "Well how did you get in there?" I ask the mad possum. "I really hate to tell you this, but you need to leave and I need to disinfect your little hidey hole. Now SHOO!" I wave my arms in all directions as the possum takes another look at the crazy human then jumps down and runs away. "Teach you to hide in my grill." Grabbing the water hose, I spray the inside of the grill then go in the house to get some disinfectant. I wasn't about to eat anything that a possum had sat on.

When I go back outside, I find Max looking at the wet grill. "What happened?"

"I found a mad possum inside when I opened the lid, so I was going to clean it." I hold up the bottle of cleaner up.

Holding a hand up, "You do not put that on a gas grill."

Dropping my arms, I watch as the takes a large wire brush from the side drawer then he scrapes the grill before wiping it down with a cloth. Turning the gas on high and letting the flames dry the inside and supposedly kill any possum germs that remained. Still wasn't sure if I was going to eat anything cooked on it.

Max sits at the table as he watches the grill, sitting beside him I ask, "How's Jacob?"

"The same. Still unconscious. So still no answers."

I fill him in on what Noah and I had discovered. He smiles as he gets up, turning the grill off before walking to the fountain. Sitting on the edge, he leans forward, studying the bottom as he lets his fingers skim the water. "So that's why we couldn't drain it. Amazing. It's going to be interesting what we find." The smile leaves his face. "You aren't going to do anything while we have guests are you?"

Sitting down beside him, watching the fish play tag with each other. "Absolutely not, there will be enough going on."

We watch the fish in silence for a few minutes, enjoying the calming effect they have. Max gets up and checks the grill before lowering the top and placing a brick on the lid. "That should keep him from opening the top until I figure something else out."

Going inside, Max heads for the den, as I start making a jug of tea. Setting the jug on the table where the sun would shine on it, I join Max in the den only to find him with the remote in his hand and his head lying against the back of the couch, he was sound asleep.

Taking the remote, I lay down on the other end of the couch and change the station before putting the remote down.

Waking later to a cat kneading at my chest, putting my hand on Felix's back, I rub him until he lays down, then I go back to sleep.

A hand was tugging on my foot, opening one eye to see Max smiling as he moves my feet off his lap, "Didn't think you needed a nap."

Stretching, "I didn't think I did either. But that felt good."

"It did." He rubs his hands together, "Now what do you say, we get cleaned up and fix our New Year's Eve dinner."

Still rubbing Felix's back, "You go ahead, I'll finish in the kitchen before I take a shower." I start to set the kitchen table and then decide it was nice enough to eat outside. For it being almost January, the weather had been extremely mild. Satisfied that the table was festive enough for a celebration with flowers and some of my best dishes, I go inside and put the potatoes and steaks on a tray for Max to take outside.

When he comes back into the kitchen, with dress pants on, a light blue dress shirt and loafers, I smile. "My goodness you look nice. I better get dressed in something besides jeans then."

Kissing him as I walk past, I head for the bathroom and smile at the thought of our first New Years. After a hot shower, I put on some light makeup, fix my hair and then decide to outdo my husband and put a dress on, something I haven't worn for a while since I found out how comfortable jeans were.

Satisfied with my appearance, I go back downstairs to find Max on the patio, drinking a glass of tea and talking on his cell. Letting him finish his conversation, I slice the bread and place it on a baking pan then take the sauces and dressing out to put on the table.

Laying his phone on the table, I notice the look on his face, something wasn't right, "What's wrong?"

"Jacob is in a coma. He has massive swelling in his brain, he may never come out of it."

I sit down and stare at my husband, "Oh no." I hold my hand out, he glances at it then nods. Taking my hand, he says a prayer for Jacob's recovery.

"Thank you. I was thinking we're worried about any answers instead of worrying about the person." Letting go of my hand, he goes to the grill and opens it then steps back and smiles. He puts his hand inside and when he brings it back out, he was holding something small. Walking over to me, he opens his hand to show me a tiny, baby possum. "This is why mama was so mad at you. She has her babies in the grill." He nods to the grill. "There are two more and I have no idea how they survived my lighting it."

"Well we won't be using that for awhile." I let my finger gently rub the top of the baby possum's head and then I hear a squeal. Both of us turn around to see mama at the edge of the yard, baring her teeth and snarling at us.

Max puts the baby back and shuts the lid. We gather everything off the table and go inside, then turn to watch mama go to the grill and run underneath it. "So that's how she got in."

We watch for a few minutes, but mama wasn't coming back out. "Guess we're cooking the steaks inside tonight."

Chapter 26

Even though the steaks would have been better fixed on the grill, our dinner was still good and satisfying. We linger at the table after we finished both of us too full to be in a hurry to clean the dishes up.

Both of us were a little quiet and I had a feeling Max was thinking about Jacob and if he would ever get any answers on Mrs. Hopkins, while I was thinking of the guests coming. And the more I thought about it, the more I was leaning toward not having an inn.

With a sigh, I get up and start cleaning the table while Max heads for the den, probably to see if the remote was working. I hear music playing softly and I smile, he had turned on the stereo. Coming to stand beside me, he helps me finish with the cleaning and then takes me in his arms and we slowly waltz around the kitchen. He turns the lights off as he guides me to the hallway and then finally into the den. I lay my head on his shoulder as we sway softly to the music, now this was a New Year's Eve party!

We dance for a while before he reaches into his pocket and pulls a piece of paper out. Handing it to me, I look at him, "What's this?"

"Well open it." He smiles. "I've never met a woman that you had to tell to open a gift."

Dropping my hands to my side, "A gift! I didn't get you anything! Did we say we were going to get each other something?"

Shaking his head, "No, just open it."

Peeling the paper open, I gasp when I see the gold necklace inside with the filigree cross that I had admired in the jewelry store several months ago, "Oh Max. It's beautiful."

He takes the necklace and puts it around my neck. I walk over to the mirror and admire the cross. Turning back around, I throw my arms around his neck, "Thank you so much. But I feel a little guilty for not getting you something."

"Darling, you give me a gift every day just by being my wife." He starts slowly dancing again, "This is nice. It's a shame we don't have dances anymore. Remember when the Moose Lodge had a dance every weekend with a live band? Those were good times."

"We never went. Matter of fact, we never did much of anything. Once Hank was home for the weekend, he wanted to stay home with me and the kids." My husband had been an insurance agent and had to travel quite a bit.

Max nods, "I remember." Looking down at me, he smiles, "I have a small bottle of champagne too, want some?"

With a smile I nod, "Hope no one finds out we're drinking."

Just as Max turns toward the kitchen, the front doorbell rings. We both look at the clock then Max scowls as he walks to the door. Taking a glance out of the side window before opening the door, "Hello, Can I help you?"

A middle-age couple was standing on the stoop. "We're sorry to bother you and we know we're a day early…oh we're the Carson's, we have a reservation."

Max looks at me over his shoulder before smiling and opening the door wider, "No problem, please come in."

The couple comes in, pulling two large suitcases and carrying two more. Just how long were they plan on staying? I hold my hand out, "Pleased to meet you, I'm Margaret Gunderson and this is my husband Max."

As the man, who I assumed was James Carson, sets the cases he was carrying down, "Again, we're sorry to come early, but we were hoping it wouldn't be an imposition."

I glance at Max and notice he was studying them and probably taking a mental note of everything about them, "That's all right. Your room is ready, so if you'll just sign in we'll show you your room and you can settle in."

Guiding them to the small desk, I pull out a card for them to fill out and lay it on top. As I hand a pen to the woman, who hadn't said a word yet, I notice the man looking at the plaque Noah had made. After she fills the card in, the man nudges her and nods toward the sign. Right then I knew that this was a hunting trip and not a stop on the way south.

"Thank you. Now if I could have your payment we'll be all set."

I wait as the woman looks at the man who was still studying the plaque. She nudges him and he turns to her, "What?"

With a soft voice, "They need the money for the room."

He looks at me and then smiles, "Oh right, sorry, we've been driving a while." He pulls his wallet out and hands me cash for the room. Waving a hand at me, "Keep the change, you'll probably deserve the tip."

My mouth immediately tightens but thankfully I keep it shut, "Thank you." Putting the money away, I get the key and walk from behind the desk, "If you'll follow me." I had made sure that we had 'no smoking' signs in several places, hoping they take notice. As I lead them upstairs, with Max following with one of their suitcases, I explain the time for lunch and the areas of the house that was available to them. Reaching their room, I open the door then step aside.

When she enters, a smile finally crosses her face, "Oh this is lovely." She lays her purse on the bed and turns to admire the room.

He enters and sets the cases he was carrying down before looking around, he didn't seem impressed. As Max sets the last of the cases down, he says, "We hope you enjoy your stay." Looking at me, I nod and head for the door.

After we close the door behind us and walk down the hall, I stop and whisper, "They aren't here for a vacation, did you see him looking at the plaque?"

Max nods and guides me to the stairs. Once we were on the ground floor, he stops, "Besides being here a day early, the plaque, paying with cash and the wife hardly saying a word...it's all suspicious."

Putting my hands on my hips, "And did you hear what he said about the change which would have been three dollars? I'd deserve it!" Raising my hands in the air as I walk to the kitchen, "That's it, no inn."

Max stops me by grabbing my arm, "Let's see how it goes first okay? I know this hasn't started off right, but we're all tired, let's see how tomorrow goes."

I nod as we lock the house and make sure everything was turned off, the desk locked and no valuables, like my purse, was out. We go upstairs quietly and into our room, after Max makes sure the cats were in the room, he shuts the door and then hugs me. "Sorry our evening was cut short."

Putting my arms around him, "It's not your fault, we'll finish after they're gone."

Chapter 27

Knowing there were other people in the house made both of us be quiet, we spoke in whispers and no shutting the bathroom door hard and we even slid the dresser drawers closed softly. Finally we both climb into bed, Max lets a breath out and closes his eyes.

I was lying against the headboard, stroking Felix's head, but thinking of our guests. Closing my eyes, I turn my thoughts to the Lord, asking for me to not judge so quickly. Max takes my hand and squeezes it before saying a soft prayer for guidance, for thankfulness and forgiveness. After he finishes, we lay quietly, each with our own thoughts, until Max says, "Did you get a copy of their ID?"

Pulling my head back, "No why, they paid in cash."

Max looks up at me, "Exactly. You need to get an ID no matter how they pay. If something happens we have their information, for insurance, for legality and just to make sure they're who they say they are."

I slap a hand to my forehead, "Margaret you're an idiot. You would think I would have thought of that."

Max laughs, "Most people would'nt now days, but it's better to be careful. See if you can get it tomorrow."

"Of course." I felt like an idiot. And it would have also given us proof of who they are. Then a thought occurs, "Maybe it would be a good idea for you to wear your badge around them, that way they'll know there's law enforcement here."

Max stares at the ceiling for a minute, "No, let's keep that quiet for now just in case they are up to something and I'll make sure the men don't wear their badges either."

"So you think something's up too?"

Turing his head to me, he nods, "Being here a night early, the look on his face when he saw the plaque and her not saying anything. I'm wondering if they're even a couple, she seems a little leery of him."

Thinking about what he said and it did seem strange that she barely spoke unless she was abused, but I didn't get that feeling. Time will tell, like starting tomorrow.

I slide down and reach over to turn the light out, letting Felix curl beside my head while Oscar grumbles from the foot and Baby was curled next to Max, "We get any more cats and we'll have to get them their own bed." Max gives me a kiss goodnight before turning the light off on his side of the bed.

Sleep was a little fitful and when the alarm clock went off, my eyes pop open and I was up. Beating Max to the bathroom, I get ready quickly and head for the stairs. At the top, I stop and listen to see if I could hear any noises from the end of the hall, but it was quiet. Hopefully they were still asleep.

Starting the coffee, I feed the cats and smile as they attack their food. Then I open the refrigerator to see what to fix for breakfast. Deciding on bacon and eggs, as I start fixing the food, I hear a loud thump from over my head which was where the guests were.

As I head for the stairs, I hear Max asking if everything was okay. Hearing a voice responding but not being able to make out the words, I wait at the foot of the stairs.

A few minutes later Max comes down the stairs wearing his trademark scowl.

"What happened?"

Max pulls me into the kitchen, "He said they dropped one of the suitcases off the bed, but I got a glimpse and saw one of the pictures on the floor. So they're looking for something."

"So we were right. By law can I just kick them out?"

Max laughs, "Well little lady, since you have the law living here, if they do any damage to the inn I can just hogtie them and shove them out the door."

Smacking him, I continue to fix breakfast, "I'm serious, it seems they're already looking so isn't that something like invasion of privacy?"

Max shakes his head, "There isn't anything in the room that's personal, now if they were looking through the desk or our room, that's a different story." Sitting down with his coffee, he takes a sip before adding, "If we find them looking in drawers or the closets, we can say something to them."

Setting a plate in front of him, he starts eating as I sit down with my coffee, "This is going to be a disaster."

Patting my hand, he says, "We don't know that yet. Let's see what happens first."

Hearing heavy footsteps coming down the stairs, I look at Max and grimace. Mr. Carson enters the kitchen and smiles, "Good morning!" He looks around, "Is there coffee?"

I get up and get a mug from the cabinet. "Cream or sugar?"

The look on his face was confusion, "Um, don't you have a tray that I can take upstairs?"

Max wipes his mouth, "We're sorry, but we only provide lunch, but you can take a couple of cups of coffee with you upstairs."

Mr. Carson gives both of us a look that plainly told us how unprofessional we were. Handing him the mugs. "You'll need to bear with us, you're the first guests we've had."

Relief spreads over his face, "Oh well, that's all right. It's a work in progress right?" Nodding at the cups, "Thank you, we'll bring the cups back down."

Once he's back upstairs, I look at Max and raise my eyebrows which makes him smile, "Maybe a pot of coffee in the morning isn't such a bad idea." After wiping his face and taking the last swig of coffee, he refills his cup and sits back down, "I'll stay until the guys get here. I want to fill them in and make them aware that they are looking around."

As he picks the paper up and starts reading it, I clean the kitchen before sitting down again. I just wasn't comfortable with people in the house, tapping the table with my hand, I was just nervous.

A hand clamps down over mine and Max lowers the paper, "Stop, it'll be all right."

Chapter 28

I turn to where I could see out the window and watch the cats as they try to catch a bird when it gets close. Hearing a light knock on the back door, I get up and let Spence and Officer Taylor in, "Good morning."

They come in, each carrying a duffle and a backpack, setting them down they both turn to Max, "Chief."

Laying the paper aside, "Good morning. Let me show you where you're going to sleep and fill you in on a couple of things."

The men pick their bags up and follow Max to the basement door. I already felt better knowing they were in the house. Finishing my coffee, I rinse the cup then lean against the sink. What to do now? I wasn't comfortable leaving the house with strangers here, I had cleaned the house, I had the laundry caught up, so what to do?

My cell phone rings, picking it up, I see Joy's face on the screen, "Good morning!"

"Hey Grams. You busy?"

"No as a matter of fact I was just wondering what I was going to do today. Our first guests arrived late last night and I'm not comfortable leaving the house." I thought I heard something in the hallway, so I walk over and see a shadow moving up the wall of the stairway. One of the Carson's had been listening.

"Good. I'm coming over and we're going to play."

I laugh, knowing that meant she wanted me to try some kind of new app or computer she had built, "Sure sweetheart, that's just what I need." And it was, whatever she wanted me to try would get my mind off the guests.

Max comes up the stairs with Spence and Taylor following, "I've told them what's happened so far and that I want them to be as visible as possible. Now I'm going to see if there's anything new with Jacob and I'll be home early." Giving me a kiss on the cheek goodbye, I watch as he leaves and immediately want him back.

Spence sits down at the table while Taylor heads down the hall and probably the den. I tell Spence that I think one of them had been listening to me on the phone.

"Don't worry Mrs. Gunderson, Chief filled us in and we know what to look for. But please get an ID so we can run it, okay?"

I nod and head for the alcove and the little desk to pull up their reservation form again. Even though I've looked at it a dozen times, I keep hoping to find something new. As I was looking over their information and the Carson's that were set to arrive in a few days, I hear footsteps again. Looking up from the computer, I see Mr. Carson. When he sees me, I sense he was hoping I wasn't around,

"Mr. Carson, I'm so sorry but I forgot to ask for an ID last night, you know the confusion. Would you mind?"

"I paid in cash so why do you need my ID?"

Spence comes in from the kitchen before I could respond, "Hey ma, want me to finish putting those cameras up?" He comes to stand beside me.

"Yes dear." I look at Mr. Carson again, "Please can I have your ID, it's required by law I'm afraid."

The look on Mr. Carson's face was enough to make me want to toss him out, "I don't have it with me. I'll give it to you later." He clears his throat, "Can you recommend a diner in town for breakfast since you didn't provide one?"

Spence steps forward which makes Mr. Carson step back and I would too. Spence is a tall, muscular man that can come across as very intimidating, "Mr. Carson is it?" He waits as Carson nods, "It is required for us to have some kind of ID, not only to protect us but you too, so if you can't provide one, we may have to ask you to leave, of course you'll get your money back minus ten percent."

Carson's face immediately went blood red, you could feel the anger radiating from him, "I will get you an ID shortly." He glares at me, "I can say that I don't think you'll be in business long with this attitude."

Spence steps forward, "That isn't your concern, we're just following the law." He crosses his massive arms across his chest which made Carson back up a step.

Turning he goes up the stairs and slams the door hard enough to jar the windows, "Oh my." I put my head in my hands. "This was a mistake."

Spence puts his hand on my shoulder, "One bad apple. I'm sure that your other guests will be fine."

Standing I shake my head, "That may be, but I'm not sure I want people I know nothing about in my home. I wonder how other inns do it? Having to share their home with strangers where they could go into any part of the house and through your things."

Heavy steps were coming back down and Carson steps into the alcove, he holds his hand out, "Here, my ID. Happy now?"

"Thank you." I take it and make a copy then hand it back to him, "I'm sorry for the confusion and thank you again."

He jerks the card out of my hand and goes back up the stairs and I wince when he slams the door again. Taking the copy of the ID out of the printer, I look at it then shake my head.

Spence looks at me, "What?"

"I would bet it's fake." Handing the sheet of paper to Spence, I watch as he studies it, "Fake right?"

Giving me a little smile, "Maybe, let me get someone on it." He takes a picture with his phone then taps the screen, handing the page back to me, "I can say he isn't 45 like that license says."

Looking at the ID again, I laugh, "And he isn't six foot three either." Dropping my hands down, I shake my head as I head for the kitchen, entering just as Joy comes in the back door, "Hello sweetheart. I hope you have something to take my mind off things."

Laying the case she was carrying in the table then looking at Spence, "Why? What's wrong?"

Sitting down, "Oh it's a long story, but basically I'm regretting opening the mansion as an inn." I notice Joy looking at Spence, "Oh this is Officer Spence, he's staying here for a few days."

Joy smiles at him, "Pleased to meet you, does Max have you under guard now?"

That makes me laugh, "Something like that."

"I'll leave you ladies and check out that ID." Spence leaves the room just as I hear footsteps on the stairs again.

Getting up, I walk to the doorway just as the Carson's open the front door and leave, slamming the door behind them. Joy comes to stand beside me, "Was that the guests?"

"Yes, they came last night as Max and I were having our New Years Eve, he's rude and demanding and I think he's been snooping upstairs. While she doesn't say a word. "

Joy wraps her arms around me, "Oh Grams, I'm sorry. I thought the idea of an inn was a good one. Maybe other guests will be better."

Giving her a smile, "It'll be all right, I have faith, if not I can unleash Margaret on them."

Joy laughs, "Sure hope they don't have to see that. Tell you what, let's get your mind off them."

Chapter 29

Sitting down at the table, I watch as Joy unzips her case and pulls a large, but slim laptop out. It was colored a bright blue and when she opens it, the keyboard had colored lights, "Goodness, that's impressive. Did you make this?"

With a huge smile, she nods, "Yes and Terry likes the concept. But I want to know what you think of the apps I added and let me know how it works for you." Placing the laptop in front of me, she walks me through a few of the features and then slides what looks like a plastic square to the side.

"What's that?"

"The mouse. You use your finger. Go ahead, just run your finger over it."

I did and watch the cursor move on the screen, "What if I want to click on something?"

"Just tap it."

I tried and sure enough I opened the mail icon, "Oh this is impressive." I play for a minute, "All right, what have you got on here?"

She shows me a few apps that basically were more for younger people than me, then she smiles, "Okay, I combined a few of the features from websites that are available from the county office, you know public records and court records, but I was also able to add DMV records." She points to an app, "Open that."

I do and see where I could fill out forms for just about anything for the county, from land records to marriage licenses. I had a thought, so I get up and get the ID copy I had made and bring it back to the table. Clicking on the DMV tab, I enter the information and immediately see a picture with the information that was a duplicate of the ID, only the picture wasn't Carson. So he had faked his ID, now I'm wondering if he's James Carson at all.

Joy watches me for a few minutes, "I think you have the gist of it, so I'll let you play. Let me know what you think." She leans over and kisses my cheek, "Thanks Grams."

"See you later dear and thank you for giving me something to do."

Wondering if I could get any more information from the DMV. I just enter James Carson and the state he had given me and then a thought, his car, the license plate, I start to get up and then remember they had left.

So instead I do another search on River Oaks and then the names Carson. Quite a few names appear, so I start at the earliest date and find that most of it was what I found earlier.

Until I come to right before the death of Mr. Cambridge. There had been papers filed disputing the ownership of the mansion from several decades before. Interesting. Moving to the court section, I find the lawsuit and smile. One of the original complainants was a Hopkins. So there must be the connection Jacob Woods thought would be his family. Searching a little more, I find two Carson's were also on the compliant. So basically they all thought they had ownership to the mansion, not knowing a codicil in Cambridge's will had stipulated who the mansion went to and when we petitioned to buy it, all of the records and deeds came in free and clear of any claims, disputes or lawsuits.

Smiling as I look further into what I could find on the Carson's, I made a mental note to Joy that this app was definitely going to come in handy. I was so engrossed in my search, I didn't know the Carson's had come back until I heard the front door slam shut. What is it with that man and doors?

Getting up, I put a smile on my face and go into the hallway, "I hope you found the diner and enjoyed your lunch."

"Lunch? More like a really late breakfast."

Stomping my foot, "Mr. Carson, I'm sorry if you find your accommodations that lacking, but if you had read the website and what we offered you would have seen that breakfast was not included. Now if you're that unhappy here, I'll be glad to give you a refund and you can leave. And if you slam another door in my house, I will definitely tell you to leave and not ask!"

Mr. Carson takes a step backward, his wife or whoever she was, who was standing behind him, slaps a hand over her mouth to hide the smile that I saw before she covered it up. But he just stares at me with an open mouth.

Spence must have heard me, because he was now standing behind me, "Everything okay?"

"Yes. I just informed Mr. Carson here of the rules of the house and I believe he's thinking it over now."

Seeing his beet red face, I was wondering if he wasn't going to blow a gasket though. Instead he lowers his head and shakes it, "You're right. I've been a little rude." He turns to look behind him at his wife, "We'll do better." I didn't know if Spence noticed the death ray that she just shot at his back, but it made me smile.

"Fine. Now I think your stay will be much better from here on." I start to turn around and nod at the clock, "Lunch will be served at 1pm and its buffet style in the dining room." I plaster a smile on my face and go back into the kitchen.

As soon as the door was shut behind me, Spence asks, "What was that about?"

"Our fine guest slamming doors and being a total pill." I turn the laptop around and show him what I had found.

He nods as he reads the report, "That's what we found out too. Whoever this guy is, he's not James Carson. I have a guy seeing if he can get an ID on the picture. The address is bogus too."

"So all the information he's given us is false?"

Spence nods at me, "I've let the chief know, but he's at the hospital right now. Jacob woke up."

Chapter 30

I clap my hands together, "Oh thank you Lord. Do you know what his condition is?"

Spence shakes his head, "No, chief just said he was awake."

Taylor comes into the kitchen, "Just got a call. It appears the picture is fake, but they came up with this."

He holds his phone so we could see the screen, on it was the man that I just fussed at and his name according to the police report that his picture was attached to is Clifford Joseph and it appears he's been arrested several times for scams, burglary and even embezzling. Huh, nice guy. I shake my head, me and my bright ideas of opening an inn.

Sitting down at the table, I let Spence take over the laptop and he smiles as he starts typing, "Wow nice laptop."

My grandmothers' pride sat up, "My granddaughter built it and she's quite good at it."

"I'll say." As he types, Taylor was tapping away on his phone so I felt a little out of place.

Getting up, I start fixing a lunch for our guests. I start to just put out some peanut butter sandwiches and let it go at that, but that would be carrying things a little too far even for me. After laying out a large platter of ham, turkey, lettuce, onions, pickles, tomatoes and cheese, I place it on the sideboard before returning to the kitchen to get the rest of 'lunch.'

Finishing with the preparations, I go to the small desk and buzz the 'Carson's' room, letting them know that there was a small buffet for lunch and they could come down anytime in the next three hours. I didn't let them know after that I was cleaning it up and there wouldn't be anything else to eat for them except the snacks in their room.

Saying a little prayer of forgiveness for being so rude myself, I wipe my hands before putting the chops we were going to have for dinner in a marinade.

Spence calls me over to the table. Sliding the laptop around he points to the screen where there was an article on Jacob Woods, it restated the incident with the young boy and also another incident with who the press said was his mother. I read the article, then frown. None of this made sense. It stated that Jacob was under suspicion of putting his mother in a coma, presumably with an insulin overdose but the doctor couldn't confirm that. It also stated that there was overwhelming evidence that Jacob was involved in a series of break ins in several small communities around the city, nothing major was taken but there was a lot of personal items stolen, like receipts, insurance papers, mortgage payments, credit cards statements, exactly things you would need for a stolen identity, to scam or even steal.

Leaning back I look at Spence, "So he may have been after something in Mrs. Hopkins' house and wasn't expecting her home. But it still doesn't explain him coming here and looking at the photos and claiming to be a distant relative of the Wright's"

Spence turns the laptop back around, "Hopefully now that he's awake we can get some answers. Let's see if we can find anything else on who's here now."

Taylor holds his hand out, "Wait, I may have something here. IT ran his picture." He hands his phone to Spence who scowls before handing the phone to me.

I study the picture then read the report that was with it. The crimes that were connected to the man were mind boggling, "How has he gotten away with so much?"

Spence nods at the phone, "Read who his lawyer was. If that's the real James Carson, he's a crook too." Turning the laptop around again for me to see.

Looking at the screen, there was a picture of a smiling man with a nice haircut, clean shaven and with a look of intelligence about him, "So that's the real James Carson?"

"One of them. Seems to be a common name, but this one has a practice where Jacob lives."

Spence takes the laptop back while he and Taylor put their heads together. Tapping the table with my hands, I really didn't have an interest in what happened before, I was concerned over what the man and woman that were here wanted. Because it sure didn't seem to be a vacation or a stop off on their way south. Especially with his attitude.

Just then there was a loud bang from upstairs. All three of us look at each other before I jump up and head for the stairs.

Chapter 31

Once I was upstairs, I head in the direction of the Carson's room then turn around, running into Taylor's chest. Regaining my footing, I head for the other end of the hallway, where my bedroom was. The door was closed, I look over my shoulder at Spence who was watching me from the middle of the hall, debating whether to follow me or Taylor. I guess I won out because he joined me as I opened the door to find dresser drawers on the floor, nightstand drawers open and the closet door open.

Someone was looking for something and the only other person in the house was Carson or Joseph, since that seems to be his real name. Fury overtaking me, I head for their room. Without bothering to knock, I push the door open to see Mrs. Carson or whoever she was laying on the bed. Walking over to her, "Where's your husband?" There wasn't a response from her. I gently touch her arm, she didn't move.

Taylor leans over and touches her neck, before opening one of her eyes. "She's been drugged." He pulls his cell out and calls for an ambulance.

Spence comes in, "There's no one on this floor. Isn't there a third floor?"

I nod and lead him to the other staircase at the end of the hallway. The door was open and we usually kept it closed. Letting Spence lead the way, we reach the top floor to see all the doors open. Spence looks at me and raises an eyebrow, I shake my head.

Letting him search the rooms before I look in each one. They had all been gone through. What in the devil was he looking for?

Not finding anyone we go back downstairs just as Max reaches the hallway, "What's going on? I heard the call for an ambulance."

"We heard a loud bang up here and found Mrs. Carson, Taylor thinks she's been drugged." Wringing my hands, hoping that she was going to be all right.

Max heads for their room just as I hear a knock at the front door. Spence goes to open the door, leaving me standing in the hallway. Watching the EMT's as they head for the room, I lean against the wall and close my eyes, saying a prayer that she will be all right. When I finish, I open my eyes and walk to the doorway to see what was happening. They were loading Mrs. Carson onto a gurney to take to the hospital.

Max comes to stand beside me, rubbing my back as he leans closer, "She'll be fine."

"It wasn't insulin was it?" Since that seems to be the choice of drug with these guys.

"I don't think so. She was coming around a little." He looks down the hall, "So they've gone through the rooms?"

I nod as fury takes over again, "You'll need to talk to Spence and Taylor, they've found out a few things."

Max nods as he follows Taylor and Spence down the stairs, while I go back to my room. Standing in the doorway, tears form in my eyes. Why do this?

This pretty much made my decision to not have an inn.

     As I clean our bedroom up, I think of what this man Joseph could be looking for and for that matter, what had brought Jacob to River Oaks. But my biggest question was why kill Mrs. Hopkins?

     Finishing getting the room back in order, I sit on the edge of the bed saying a silent prayer for answers. The bottom of the bedspread moves and slowly three cats emerge from underneath. They all jump up beside me and I pull them close, "Sorry guys, I know that man scared you and if I have anything to do with it, he'll be gone soon."

     With a sigh, I get up and go through the other rooms, putting things back in order and making sure that nothing had been broken. When I get to the last room on the top floor, I almost start to cry. We had put a large painting on the wall of the Cambridge's, we had found the painting in this room, so we had left it here but it now had slash marks. The painting was ruined.

     As I turn to leave the room, Clifford Joseph was standing in the doorway and just from the look on his face, he was furious. He takes a step toward me but I stand my ground, "What have you done to my house? Just what are you looking for?"

     He smiles, a very unpleasant smile, "Well Mrs. Gunderson, you should know what I want. A treasure was left in this house. Well maybe not a treasure to most people, but to me it's priceless." He steps closer, "You people redid the whole house so I know you found it."

My hands go to my hips, "Just what is it you're looking for, because I have no idea."

He laughs, but it was more a snort, "Oh you know exactly what I want." He steps closer, his face only inches away from mine, "And if you don't hand it over, well, I won't be nice."

I didn't back down, "What did you do to your wife, or whoever she is?"

Tilting his head back, he laughs more, "My wife! I wouldn't marry that woman if you paid me. She's supposed to be an actress, but so far she hasn't done a thing I told her too." He motions toward the door, "Lead the way and you better take me to the treasure."

Crossing my arms, I shake my head, "I have no idea what you're looking for so how am I supposed to lead you to it?" I say a silent prayer, asking God for help and guidance.

Studying my face for a minute, he scowls, "You really don't know what I want do you?" Running his hands through his hair, he paces for a minute, "All right. Show me what you found in the house when you took it over."

Shaking my head, "We didn't find anything except a few picture albums, books, a few knick knacks and some furniture." I wasn't about to tell him of the other things I had locked in the cabinet, but as far as I could remember, none of it was valuable.

"You mean that stuff in the den?"

When I nod my head, he balls a fist and hits the wall making a huge hole.

"Now look here…"

He turns to face me, his fist still balled and ready to strike out. Even though my heart rate went up, I stood my ground, trying to not let him see my fear.

With a growl, he turns, leaving the room and then I hear footsteps pounding down the stairs. After hearing the front door slam, I let out the breath I had been holding and sit on the bed. Felix jumps on my lap and yeows, pulling her close, I lay my head on top of his, "Were you watching after me? Were you going to attack if that man did anything?" His heavy purring answered my question.

With Felix in my arms, I go back downstairs to give him a treat before putting him on the floor. Getting a bottle of water, I sit down at the table and take a drink, noticing that I was shaking.

Chapter 32

Max, Spence and Taylor find me still sitting at the table an hour later when they come back. Max takes one look at me, "What happened?" He takes my hand as he sits down beside me.

I relate cleaning the house, finding the painting destroyed and then Clifford Joseph showing up and what he wanted.

"What treasure? We didn't find anything except family mementos."

Nodding as I agree with him, "I know. So I have no idea what he's talking about." Then I remembered where they had been, "How's the woman? He told me she was an actress he'd paid."

Max nods, "She came to on the way to the hospital. Once she was in a room, she told us everything she knew, which isn't anything that will help us."

I hadn't been paying attention to Spence and Taylor until I smell meat cooking. Looking into the kitchen to see both men busy preparing dinner. I start to get up, but Max holds me back and smiles, "Let them, they're both pretty good cooks."

With a half-smile, I nod before asking, "So what did she say?"

Leaning back, he frowns, "Nothing that really made any sense. She said that she was hired to play a part. She was to pretend she was Joseph's wife, but to not say anything. According to the amount of money that was mentioned, she agreed but when he started tearing the room up and she complained is when he must have slipped her something."

My finger starts tapping the table, "Wonder what kind of money he has?" I pull the laptop over and type in Clifford Joseph's name, scrolling through what was posted about him. Hearing Max talking I look over and he gives me a wink, he was getting a warrant for his bank account.

Spence starts carrying plates and silverware to the table, I shut the laptop and start to get up to help but Spence puts a hand on my shoulder, "We got this."

Letting the guys take over, I turn back to the article I had found about the foreclosure proceedings on Joseph's house and the only reason there was an article is because he pretty much tore the bank up, hit the manager and threatened to burn the bank down if they took his house. Shaking my head, "This man needs to be locked up."

"Why?" Max looks over to see what I was looking at.

Pointing to the article, "Seems as if he almost destroyed the bank when they foreclosed on his house." I look at Max, "He's slammed doors and gone through every room in the house that he could. He's dangerous and now gone to who knows where after drugging someone he was supposedly paying to be his wife."

Rubbing his face, "Until he actually does damage and since he's a guest in the house, he can say he was only looking around."

"What about the painting and what about that woman?"

Max leans back as the guys place the food on the table, "Wait." With a smile he adds, "I know

that's hard for you, but in this case we actually
need to if we have any hope of charging him with
anything."

Spence and Taylor sit down and start to spoon
food on their plates when Max clears his throat,
taking my hand, he bows his head and prays for
healing of the woman and Jacob and a solution to our
problem, then giving thanks for all our blessings.
After saying Amen he nods to the guys to let them
know they could go ahead.

We're quiet as we fill our plates, each in our
own thoughts. Laying my fork down, I look over at
Max, "Is there any way to just kick him out and be
done with it?"

Shrugging Max says, "Sure, but I'd really like
to catch him. With his record, I'd really like to
get him on something solid. Drugging the woman is
something, but not enough to hold him. I'm hoping
he's connected to Jacob and we can get him as an
accomplice."

I nod, understanding what he was saying. But I
wasn't going to be comfortable in my own home with
him here. Hearing the back door open, I turn to see
Noah coming into the house. Smiling, "Hey Noah. Get
a plate and join us."

Noah comes into the room and Max introduces
him to Spence and Taylor as he sits down. Nodding to
both men, he lays a flash drive on the table as he
reaches for the laptop, "I may have found
something." After loading whatever he had, he turns
the laptop our way. A video starts of Jacob walking
down the street that Mrs. Hopkins lives on, we watch
as he walks past the house, stops, then continues
on. A sedan pulls beside him and he talks to the

driver before turning back to the house and walking
around the house. The video stops and Noah looks at
Max, "This video is from a homeowner. After he heard
what had happened he knew he needed to turn it in,
but didn't want to talk to you." He smiles at Max.

"Let me guess, Mr. Webber." Max smiles before
turning to me, "You know him, John Webber, we got
into a little shouting match a couple of decades ago
about his parking in the loading zone at his store."
Shaking his head, "He's never gotten over the
tickets I gave him."

I smile at the memory, the whole town talked
about it for weeks until John Webber realized that
Max wasn't going to back down and finally paid the
tickets, but only after his car was towed. Letting
the memory fade, I nod at the computer, "So is that
Clifford Joseph in the car?"

Spence nods, "Sure looks like him." He glances
at me, "By chance do guests have to list their cars
when they check in?"

Rubbing my forehead at something else I didn't
think about, "No they don't." Looking at Max, "This
is the first and last guest we're going to have."

With a smile, Max takes my hand, "I wanted you
to find out on your own how hard running an inn is.
And yes this can be the last guest." Turning to
Spence, "We need to find the vehicle, can you get a
plate from the video?"

Taylor pulls the laptop closer and runs
through it again, "I think we have enough to start
since we know the make and model. Can I take this
down to the station?" Getting nods from both Noah

and Max, he takes the flash drive and excuses himself.

My appetite was gone, so I push my plate away which Noah immediately takes. With a smile at my friend, I sip my tea and wonder how we were going to get anything on this Clifford Joseph.

Chapter 33

      After everyone had finished their meal, Max joins the guys as they discuss Jacob, Clifford Joseph and the woman while Noah and I clean the kitchen, he comes to stand close to me.

      "Tell me what's been going on." He leans against the counter as he dries the dishes.

      I fill him in on finding the woman unconscious and what Clifford Joseph had done to the rooms upstairs and the painting "I also found out that he's lost his house and hurt the bank manager over it. They're running his financials. But what I don't understand is this treasure he keeps saying is in the house."

      Noah gives me a half smile, "Think it could be what's in the fountain?"

      I drop the dish I was washing, "I forgot all about that." Looking behind me, "But we can't look while that man is here."

      "You may not be able to, but I can." He finishes drying the dishes and puts them away, "I can do it either when he isn't here or pretend I'm working on the fountain," He pats my shoulder, "And have Blackie close by in case he gets nosy on what I'm doing." Blackie was his horse and had a certain instinct about people, he wasn't going to let Joseph get anywhere near where Noah was.

      Smiling at my neighbor, "Just don't get caught. You still have the key?"

      Nodding as he heads for the door, "I do and it's in a safe place." He leaves, giving me a little hope that he'll find something and this will all be over and I can get my house back. Oh that wasn't nice, was it Lord?

Finishing the kitchen, I take one more look around to make sure everything was put up before cutting the overhead light out. Going in search of the men, I find them in the den, all of them with a laptop and their cell phones, "Need anything?"

They all look up then shake their heads, "No Maggie, we're good. Did you want to watch TV? We can go downstairs."

Before I could answer, I hear a loud bang. Someone just slammed the front door. Max gets up and heads for the hallway with Spence and Taylor standing just inside the door, "Mr. Carson, we had no way to get in touch with you, but your wife is in the hospital."

Clifford Joseph stands there and stares at Max for a moment, "What? What happened? Did you do something to her?" He glares at me.

Max takes a step forward before I had a chance to open my mouth and to ice the cake, he pulls his badge out for Joseph to see, "Sir, to be honest, we've had just about enough of your accusations and rudeness. No, your wife appears to have been drugged, know anything about that?"

Clifford Joseph takes a good look at the badge, glances at me then turns and leaves, quickly. I watch as Max shuts the door and locks it, "Aren't you going after him?"

"On what charges? We don't have proof of anything."

Max goes back into the den, leaving me standing there fuming. I was half tempted to go after Joseph but had a better idea. Opening the door, I watch as Joseph tears down the driveway, giving me just enough time to get the first three letters of his license plate and the model of the car. Then I grumble when I see the ruts he had made in the driveway, "That man has no manners whatsoever."

Stomping back inside, I go to the den, "ZXC, and it's a dull silver Toyota sedan."

Spence and Max smile and Taylor starts typing. Spence looks at Max, "I still want to know why she isn't a detective instead of just a consultant."

Max smiles at me with a wink, "She gets in enough trouble just being a consultant, I can't imagine what she would do as a full-fledged detective."

"Oh ha ha. Since you are here, I'm leaving for a while. I need a break." Leaving the men to do their investigation, I grab my purse and keys and leave the mansion, taking a deep breath as I shut the back door behind me.

As I get into my little bug I smile, it wasn't that long ago that I would stay home all the time and not think anything about it. Now…now I needed to get out and see people. What a change Lord and thank you!

Chapter 34

After bumping down the driveway thanks to the ruts Clifford Joseph had made, I reach the road and stop. Where to go? Oh who cares, I just needed to get out, so I drive aimlessly down the mountain and around town until I see Elsie coming out of the diner. Stopping beside her, I roll the window down, "Hey Elsie."

She leans down so she could see me, "Well Margaret, just where have you been for days?" She opens the car door and gets in.

Pulling away from the curb, "I've been home. This first guest is a pain. I didn't want to leave him in the house alone because frankly I don't trust him." I wasn't about to tell her what had been happening, she'd have it all over town in minutes.

"Well that's a bummer. What's he been doing?"

"Slamming doors and rearranging things."

"Of all the nerve! Hopefully your other guests won't be like that."

I slow down when I see a grey sedan parked in front of the one bar that was in downtown River Oaks. Checking the license plate, yes it was Joseph and I wanted to watch him, just to see what he did.

Pulling my car in the lot of the antique store that was across the street, I park then turn to Elsie, "I want to watch this guy and I need you to promise to not say a word to anyone on what we were doing."

Elsie eyes me for a minute then grins, "Care to tell me what he did?"

"He's just plain rude and if he comes out of there stumbling, I'm calling it in and maybe he'll have to sleep it off in jail."

"Wow you really don't like this guy do you?" She smiles at me than pats my hand, "No I won't say anything since it seems the worst he's doing is drinking." She settles in her seat then digs in her enormous bag until she pulls a pair of binoculars out.

"What don't you have in there?"

"A gun. I'd have one of those if your husband hadn't taken it away from me." Max had confiscated her little handgun when it went off in the casino we had been checking out.

I raise an eyebrow at her before turning my attention back to the bar. It seems to be a pretty busy place, several men had walked in just in the few minutes we had been sitting here. I recognized a few and so did Elsie because she started commenting on what their wives would say and she wasn't surprised to see a few of them.

I sit patiently wondering how long he would stay in there when I see the door open and a man come out. It was Clifford Joseph, "That's him."

Elsie raises the binoculars and watches him for a minute, "Why are you watching Edward Wright?"

Jerking my head in her direction, "Who?"

"Edward Wright. His family was one of the first in town, well his father worked with yours at the shop." She points toward Joseph, "He married a cousin of one of the Cambridge's, he's supposed to be some big shot accountant up in Northern Virginia somewhere."

Looking back at Joseph slash Carson slash Wright and start to wonder just what he was really up too? "I need to talk to Max. Were you going home? I can give you a ride."

"Sure that would be nice. Aren't you going to find out where he's going?"

Watching as he stumbles getting into his car and think that may be a good idea, "Yes, let's just see where goes then I'll take you home."

Starting my car, I wait as he pulls out, barely missing the car in front of him. We follow at a good distance as he starts out of town then pulls into the parking lot of a motel at the edge of town. Pulling across the street, I watch as he stumbles up the stairs and unlocks the door of a room, "Now why is he staying here if he has a room at the mansion?"

I watch for a few more minutes then head back to town to drop Elsie off before talking to Max. There was something going on besides the man just wanting some kind of treasure. And I was determined to find out what.

Pulling into Elsie's driveway, she sits for a minute before saying, "I know something else is going on, but you'll tell me in good time." She looks at me, "Unless you want me to help you with surveillance, you know I'm good at it." She gives me a little smile.

"I know and I thank you. But this is something Max is looking into so I need to step back a little."

Elsie opens the door and gets out then leans down, "I'm excited to hear the new pastor Sunday. Have you heard anything else about Tom?"

Shaking my head, "Not really. Only that he was doing better. And yes, I'm looking forward to hearing the new pastor too."

She shuts the door and after making sure she gets inside, I call Max, "Maggie, you haven't been gone long enough to get in trouble."

"No I haven't but listen, I had Elsie with me when we saw Joseph come out of the bar downtown, she said his name was Edward Wright and he was an accountant, so for curiosity I followed him to the motel right outside of town and it seems he has a room there too."

"Well that's interesting. I'll keep Taylor here and Spence and I will check it out, don't you do anything." By his tone, he meant what he was saying.

"I'm not, I'm going to go by the bookstore and maybe the church for a few minutes."

"Be careful, see you later."

Hanging up, I start to head back to the motel and watch then decide that Max was probably going to send someone there, so I actually do head for the bookstore.

Chapter 35

After walking the aisles in the bookstore for several minutes without picking a book up since my mind was on whoever the man was, I decide to head back home.

Seeing Noah scraping the gravel back into the ruts in the driveway, I stop, "How come you're straightening the driveway?"

Leaning on the rake, he smiles, "Maybe because I didn't want my truck bumping in these holes." When he sees my look, he adds, "I offered too since it seems Max has his mind on your visitor."

"I followed him to a motel at the edge of town, seems he has a room there too." I get out and lean against my car, "That's suspicious to me."

Noah leans beside me, "That it is." He's quiet for a moment, "But it may be a good time to check out the fountain."

As I think about it, I smile, "It is because he's sleeping off an afternoon at the bar." Getting back in my car, I park in the garage as Noah puts the rake up and walks through the hedges to his house.

Going inside, I change into my garden clothes, pull some wet boots on and head back outside just as Noah reaches the fountain. We stand and stare at the fish for a minute, "Think we should leave the fish or put them in a tub?"

Noah looks around then grabs the barrel he collects rain water in and dumps most of it out. Catching the fish to move them was a different story until Noah retrieves a fishing net from the garage.

Resting on the edge after we finish, I watch Noah put a small bucket, a handled scrub brush, pulls the hose out and sets a container of soap down, then I understood what he was doing, "Good idea, if anyone comes along, we're cleaning the fountain."

"I always knew you were smart." Rolling his pants leg up, he carefully steps into the fountain. Walking to the faucet, he opens the drain lever and we watch as the water slowly drains out. Once there was only an inch or so left, he goes to the grate in the floor and studies it.

Reaching in his pocket, he pulls the key out then winks at me while I say a silent prayer that this was going to be good news.

Fitting the ornate key into the lock, he turns the key and pulls the grate out. Settling on his knees, he leans down with a flashlight, looking into the hole.

"I want to see." I make my way to him and bend over to where I could see inside the opening. There was another piece of what appears to be granite with another keyhole. Fitting the key into the hole, he turns the key but it seems an extra strong hand needed to turn the key, but he finally got it, raising the slab out and setting it aside, we turn back to the hole.

There appears to be a small box inside. Noah reaches in and pulls the box out. It was small, maybe about ten inches square and my hands were itching for Noah to hurry up and open it. Wiping his hands on his jeans, he slowly slides the box open and we both just look inside.

Reaching in, I pull a small burlap bag out and open it. Inside were several chalky looking rocks, I start to toss them down when Noah grabs my hand, in a whisper he says, "Those are uncut diamonds."

With a deep swallow, I put the diamonds back in the bag and tuck it in my pocket.

Noah reaches in the box again, this time he pulls out several folded pieces of paper. Just as he was getting ready to open them, we hear a noise from the mansion. We quickly put the box back in the hole, the lid back over it and then get the grate back in and locked just as the back door opens and the woman that was pretending to be Carson's wife comes out carrying her suitcase.

Noah pretends to be working on the pipes at the faucet as she walks over with a smile, "Hi, I just wanted to say goodbye and thanks for everything, especially finding me."

I step out of the fountain and meet her before she got too close, "Oh my dear, it was nothing. I'm glad that you're all right. How will you get home?"

She nods toward the house, "I have a cab waiting. But I didn't want to leave without seeing you. Your husband said it was all right for me to leave but he may have more questions later."

I nod, "Yes they do that sometimes. I'm so sorry that you were misled."

Shaking her head, "It was my own fault, I heard the amount he was going to pay and didn't think anything through. Trust me, when I get home I'll be finding a job."

Patting her shoulder, "Well good luck and I wish you well."

With a smile and a nod, she picks up her case and walks around the side of the house. I let a breath out then rejoin Noah. He had everything back in place and water was running back into the fountain. We get the fish back in and put everything back before going inside the house.

Kicking my boots off, I head for the sink and wash my hands as Noah leans against the counter and pulls the piece of paper out. Spreading it out, we find that it had been a letter of some kind, but the ink had faded so much that the words couldn't be made out.

With a sigh, "We may never know what that said." I pull the bag out of my pocket and let the diamonds slide into my palm. If one didn't know what they were, it would seem to be just milky rocks, "We need to put these somewhere safe and I really don't want to leave them here with that character running loose."

"I have a place, that is if you trust me enough."

Giving Noah a glare that should be able to melt the diamonds I was holding, "I can't believe you said that."

He gives me a broad smile, "Well hello Margaret, wondered where you'd been lately."

Smacking him on the shoulder, I hand him the diamonds when I hear the front door open. He quickly tucks them away as I open the refrigerator and got us both bottles of water.

When we hear the footsteps going upstairs, I grimace, "Guess he's back."

"Are you going to be okay?"

Nodding, "Yes, Taylor is supposed to be here somewhere, probably in the basement."

With a nod, he turns, "Call me if you need me."

After he leaves, I start working on dinner, wondering why Carson, Joseph, Wright bothered to come back.

Chapter 36

I was so busy concentrating on what our guest was up to that I never heard someone come into the kitchen until I was pushed against the counter.

"Since we're alone right now, I want to know where the treasure is and this time you're going to tell me."

The counter was digging into my waist, making it hard to breath, "I don't know what treasure you're talking about." I manage to croak out.

A hand wraps around my arm, tightly and pulls me away from the kitchen counter, "Show me what you've found in the house."

Shaking my head as he pulls me toward the doorway, "There's nothing but knick knacks and some photos." Pushing me as we reach the hallway, I stumble and fall against the wall. Turning to look up at the man and the look on his face was pure desperation. I may be in trouble here.

Pulling me to my feet then pushing me again, "Show me. NOW!"

Shaking, I walk into the den and over to the corner I had dedicated to the Cambridge's. I point at the wall where the pictures were hanging and the cabinet which held little trinkets we had found around the house, "That's it."

His eyes roam over the paintings and then the cabinet before turning to me, "There's more than this. Now show me."

Raising my hands, "That's all we found, if there was something before we bought the house, I don't know where it could be."

Rubbing his hand over his face, then through his hair, I could tell he was going to do something. Before I had a chance to make a move, he pulls me to the front door as he starts to push me out the door, I deliberately stumble and make the small chair fall over, hoping the noise will alert Taylor.

Grabbing the back of my shirt, he practically drags me to his car and pushes me into the front seat. I try to get out as he gets in the driver's seat, but suddenly there was a gun pointed at me.

Turning my head, I see Taylor coming out the door with his phone to his ear.

As the car speeds down the driveway, spewing the gravel that Noah had raked back, I grab the dashboard to keep from sliding, "Where do you think you're taking me? My husband will have every road blocked in just a few minutes."

He shakes his head, "He won't find us or me. You're going to tell me everything you know about that house and the Cambridge's and it better be the truth."

I give up trying to explain to this idiot that I didn't know anything more that what he just saw, because he had it in his head there was some kind of valuable treasure. I had to keep from smiling as I think about the diamonds. Then I close my eyes and concentrate on the Lord and pray for safety and help for this man.

As he speeds down the road, I start to smile and think of him speeding through town. They'll catch him in a heartbeat and if he's going back to the motel, he may be greeted there too.

But he turns and heads in the opposite direction from town and the other room he had. Where was he taking me, the closest town this way was forty five minutes away and it was windy mountain road the whole way. Oh Lord.

Clinching my hands together as the takes the turns too fast, hoping that he can keep control of the car, he suddenly hits the brakes and turns off the road. Was he taking me to the river, because that was the only thing at the end of this road.

Slowing down on the dirt road, he guides the car down the rutted road, thank goodness. Then I see an RV parked beside the river bank. How many places did this man have to stay at?

Stopping the car, he gets out and pulls my door open, "Get out."

"What if I don't want too?"

Reaching in, he grabs me by the arm and pulls me out. Stumbling, he pushes me toward the RV and into a chair. Picking up some rope, he ties my wrists to the armrests before going inside the RV. A flashback to John Tom at his camper behind the church several years makes my heartrate go up.

Pulling at the restraints, they were a little loose but not enough for me to slide my arms out. But as I start to try, he comes back out of the RV carrying a drink.

Turning the other chair to where he could see the road, he sits down and takes a deep drink. The

gun was tucked in his waistband and I could see a
sheath holding a knife beside it.

Margaret I believe you may be in trouble.

Chapter 37

Finishing that drink, he gets up and goes inside coming back with another one. Well if he gets drunk, I have a chance of getting away from him.

After taking another sip, he clears his throat, "I was denied an inheritance that was due me. That's what I'm looking for."

"Care to tell me exactly what that inheritance is?"

Turning his head to look at me, then getting up and moving his chair so he could talk to me face to face, "I'm sure you know the whole story of the Cambridge's, or at least what you could find out. But there was another family, the Wright's, who also had a part of the property. Mind you it wasn't much, just a little house on the same property, but they did the work. They kept the gardens, they cooked and cleaned the mansion."

"In other words they were the help." So why would they be entitled to an inheritance?

He nods, "Basically, but Mr. Wright helped Cambridge with his business too and in my opinion, if it wasn't for him, it would have tanked." He drains the glass then gets up going inside for another one. At this rate he'll be drunk before I have any answers.

When he comes out and sits down, I ask, "By the way, exactly what is your name? I've heard James Carson, Clifford Joseph and Edward Wright."

With a smile and a wink, he says, "All of them. I was born James Carson but not related to the other Carson's, then I changed my identity to Edward

Wright after the mess with the Cambridge's and yes I was in town under that name. But after the last Cambridge died I moved north and changed my name again and began a pretty lucrative accounting business until my past came knocking on the door." He takes a deep gulp of his drink.

"Jacob Woods."

His face hardens, "Yes, dear ole Jacob. How he found out that the Wright's didn't have a son and were nothing but servants and that his last relative was a distant relation, I have no idea. But the man totally screwed things up. That's one reason I came back to see if I could get the treasure that the Cambridge's proclaimed. If I got to it first, I could claim it and be done with it and be well off the rest of my life." With that he smiles.

"You do realize the so called treasure were the roses they had cultivated don't you?" I had managed to slip one thumb loose from my bindings.

He waves a hand at me, "Oh that's hogwash. How could a rose be a treasure? It's got to be money or something valuable and I intend to get it if I have to tear that mansion apart." His eyes were drooping and his speech was starting to slur.

Come on, get up and get another drink, I think maybe one or two more and he'll pass out, "They're considered a treasure because they are a hybrid of two very famous roses and have won a few awards."

Shaking his head and giving a snort, "Yeah right. I'm supposed to believe that a rose won an award and was made famous."

"Look it up, it's all documented." I had one
hand loose now, but I keep my hands behind me and
say a prayer that I can get away.

He pushes himself up and takes a few stumbles
before reaching the RV door, he misses the first
step as he enters the trailer. I wait to see what
will happen when he comes out. Holding onto the door
frame he steps down, almost missing the step.
Reaching his chair, he almost turns it over as he
holds on to it to sit down. Once seated, he takes a
deep drink, his head bobbing in every direction.
Squinting at me, "What were we talking about?"

"Your accounting business." I had both hands
loose and was ready to run as soon as that head
drops.

Giving a half nod, "Right." His speech was so
slurred now I couldn't make out what he was saying,
"Good business." He taps his head, "Cause I'm
smartest man ever." His head droops, the glass falls
out of his hands and I wait.

After several minutes, he starts snoring and I
was immediately glad I didn't have to listen to
that, my gosh it was loud! Getting up, I look at his
car and think of taking it and then decide if he
wakes up maybe he won't remember me being here so I
head for the river and hope that the trail that used
to run beside it was still there.

Chapter 38

Glad that I had tennis shoes on, I reach the river and look upstream and smile. It appears that the trail was used regularly because it was a clean path. Walking the trail, I have to step over a couple of fallen trees but other than that, it was an easy walk.

Stopping to rest, I sit on a fallen tree and watch the river as it flows over the rocks and watch the birds dipping their heads in the water. If I wasn't getting away from an idiot, I would enjoy this.

"Help me get there Lord." I get up and continue walking, finally reaching the fork where the river flows to the west and then into town. It didn't take long to get to the first house, which belonged to Jack and Sylvia Lamb. It was a long ranch with beige siding, a dark grey slate roof and a porch that wrapped around the whole house.

Walking the path from the river to their yard, I hear music coming from the garage where I find Jack singing along as he works on a mower. Knocking on the side of the garage, I yell, "Hey Jack!"

Raising his head, he smiles when he sees me then cuts the music down, "Margaret! What brings you out here?"

"Oh I had car trouble up the road and was wondering if I could use your phone."

"Well sure, but I'd be glad to look at your car. That's an awful new car to be breaking down." A frown crosses his face as he hands me his cell phone.

"Thanks. I'll only be a minute." Stepping away from the garage, I call Max.

"Maggie, where are you and are you okay?"

"I'm fine. I'm at the Lamb's house. And I'll fill you in when you get here."

"Are you hurt?" I could hear his feet clumping on the floor as he talks.

"I'm fine, but I have some information and you may want to get a couple of cruisers ready. Right now he's passed out, he has an RV parked at the old road where the fishing hut used to be."

Hearing his truck starting, "I'm on my way to get you and I'll get a couple of men over there."

Handing the phone back to Jack, "Thank you. Max will be here in a few minutes."

Reaching in a small refrigerator, he pulls a bottle of water out and hands it to me, "Sure you don't want me to look at your car?"

Taking a sip of water, "Thank you, but no it's all right, Max knows exactly what to do. How's Sylvia?"

"She's fine and looking forward to hear the new preacher." Shaking his head, "Really sorry to hear about Tom and sure hope he gets better. Such a great pastor."

Nodding, "I agree and just keep praying that he does get better. But I think the interim pastor will be a good fit for us. He seems really excited to have this chance." Feeling something rubbing against my leg, I look down to see a large tabby cat, "Well hello pretty." I look up at Jack, "What's her name?"

"Cleo. She just showed up one day, had a litter of kittens the next day and has been here ever since." Just then several small kittens run over to the mama and start climbing all over her.

Laughing I pick one up and snuggle the tiny, orange kitten, "Oh they're so sweet! And my cats are going to have a fit when I come home smelling like another cat." Getting a nuzzle under my chin as I stroke the kitten's back. I hear a truck coming. Looking over my shoulder to see Max, "Oh there's Max." Setting the kitten back on the ground then rubbing the mama's head for a second before turning to Max.

Holding his hand out, "Hello Jack, good to see you. Hope my wife wasn't any trouble."

"Not at all, glad to help. I offered to help her with the car but she said you knew what to do."

Max looks at me, I give him a wink before he answers, "Yeah it's just a little finicky, just need to hold your mouth right sometimes."

Jack laughs, "Understand. See you Sunday."

Thanking Jack again, we walk toward the truck. After getting in and buckling the seat belt, Max looks at me, "Tell me."

I fill him in on all that had happened and what Carson/Joseph/ Wright had done and said, Max grumbles, "The man is delusional. But I'm glad you're all right."

Max turns onto the road to the RV and slows down as he approaches, seeing two cruisers parked with the officers leaning on their cars. I knew the man was probably still passed out and they couldn't rouse him. When Max walks up with me behind me, he stands and stares at the RV, "Is he inside?"

One of the officers shakes his head, "When we got here, the chairs were overturned, the door open, but no one here."

Chapter 39

Well great, "Maybe I shouldn't have left him."

Max shakes his head, "No you did the right thing getting away from him." Looking around then at me, "Which way did you go?"

Nodding at the path, "I took the trail beside the river."

"Okay men, let's spread out, two of you take the path and we'll check around here."

The men head for the path, while Max searches around the RV and I go inside. There had to be something inside that will give us a clue of some sort.

Entering the RV, the first thing I notice is the smell. Wrinkling my nose, I leave the door open to get some fresh air. There were several liquor bottles on the counter, along with a pile of glasses in the small sink. There weren't any personal items lying around, I was hoping for a pile of papers that detailed what he was after.

Taking in the table and the rest of the countertop, there wasn't anything except trash. Fast food wrappers, plastic cups, empty chip bags, the man definitely had a lousy diet.

Entering the bedroom, "Oh my word." I thought the odor in the front was bad, but mercy. Holding my nose, I look at the nasty bed that looks as if it hadn't been changed in months then turn my attention to the dresser. There wasn't anything in the drawers, the closet had a few shirts hanging and a pile of dirty clothes on the floor.

Leaving the smelly room, I head for the front and take in the trash on the floorboard before my attention goes to the dashboard and the papers. There were gas receipts, a few hotel receipts and a map of River Oaks. An old map, this one didn't have the interstate that ran beside River Oaks on it.

As I rummage through the rest of the debris, Max comes in, "Lord have mercy, what a smell." He wrinkles his nose.

"Pleasant isn't it?"

"We're both going to need showers after this. Find anything?" He comes to stand beside me.

"An old map and some receipts and from the dates on these, he's been here for a couple of weeks. This one is dated the day Mrs. Hopkins was killed from Ed's station." Handing them to Max, I go through the rest of the trash and find a letter, "Wait here's a letter."

Unfolding the paper, the first thing I notice is the monogram at the top. It was a large, filigreed C, so maybe the Cambridge's stationary. Reading the letter was a little difficult since the ink had faded, but basically it said that the services of the Wright's were no longer needed after the death of James Cambridge's wife, "It appears to be a letter dismissing the services of the Wright's. Wonder why he has this?"

"A question for him when we find him." Max takes the letter and tucks it in his pocket. Turning around, "Let's get out of here before the odor kills our sense of smell."

Leaving the RV, we both take deep breaths when we get outside. Then I notice the car was gone, "Max his car is gone."

Max whips his head up and glares at the place where the car had been parked, "Well that's great."

Radioing the officers, Max heads for his pickup then turns to look at me, "Come on, I'll drop you at the house and then start searching for him."

Getting in the truck, I wonder where he could have gone unless it was back to the mansion, "Is Taylor still at the mansion?"

"Yes and Spence too. Taylor feels really bad for this so don't give him a hard time. He said if you hadn't turned the chair over, he never would have heard you."

Waving my hand, "I understand. I won't say anything, it isn't his fault. And I'm fine."

Max pulls beside the mansion and looks at me, "Stay close to the guys and I'll be back as soon as I can." Giving me a light kiss, I get out and watch as he turns around and leaves.

"What's going on?"

I turn to see Noah standing behind me, "Oh it's a long story and I need something to eat. Come inside and I'll fill you in."

Chapter 40

Once we were in the kitchen and fixing some
sandwiches, I tell Noah everything that had
happened. Sitting down at the table, I ask Noah, "Do
you think he's after the diamonds?"

Noah takes a bite of his sandwich before
answering me, "I don't think so. I don't think he
really knows what he's looking for. He's under the
impression that the Cambridge's were rich and we
know they were well off, but not rich. We know the
Wright's worked for them, but not relations. The
Carson's were friends only, and Carson worked at the
plant. They all worked and after Mrs. Cambridge
died, James Cambridge gave up. Everything. So there
wasn't any income coming in."

Taking in everything he had said some pieces
were starting to fit together. I was beginning to
think that Carson/ Joseph / Wright, besides being
delusional, was looking for a legend that didn't
exist, "Do you have the little case the key was in?"

"I put it back in the den with a different key
in it, I have the original hidden in the barn."

Getting up, I go into the den and open the
curio cabinet and get the key box. Taking it back to
the kitchen with me, I sit down and study the case
for a minute before opening it. It was small, just
big enough to hold the ornate key in a small padded,
fitted bed of velvet. Rubbing the velvet with my
finger, I feel a little bump. Lifting the key Noah
had put in, I push at the small bump and the bottom
pops up. Looking at Noah, I smile before turning the
case upside down, the bottom falls out along with a
small piece of paper. Lifting it carefully, I unfold
it and smile. There was the filigreed 'C' again, it

was from the Carson's. I start reading, "To whomever finds this missive has found the treasure of the Cambridge Manor. A treasure that has been passed down through several ancestors. It is our desire that when this is found, no matter what decade to use it for their own pleasure and not for evil. With sincerity and a joy of passing the treasure on." There was a signature at the bottom, but I couldn't make the name out, sliding the paper over the Noah, "Can you make the name out?

He studies the paper for a minute, "I think the first name is Thomas but I can't make the last name out." He takes a picture of the paper with his cell before carefully folding it up and putting it back in the box then tucking the bottom back in, "Who knew there were so many secrets with this house?"

Shaking my head, "It's mind boggling. The biggest secret in my old house was how to get the basement door open because it always stuck."

Noah laughs as he picks our plates up and carries them to the sink, "I'm going to do some more research, especially on Joseph or whatever his name is." Noah had worked for the government at one time, he never would tell in what capacity, but the man could find out anything about anyone, including things they probably didn't know about themselves, "Thanks for lunch and try not to get into any more trouble today."

"Bye Noah and thanks." I gaze out the window and think of the diamonds and wonder why they never used them for their own money problems or maybe they didn't have problems. Letting my mind wonder, then realize I was thinking of the woman in Mark with the two small copper coins putting them in the temple treasury, Jesus tells everyone that she put in all she had. Was that what the Cambridge's had done? Put all they had in the fountain?

With a sigh, I get up and finish cleaning the kitchen. Hearing a throat clearing behind me, I turn and smile at Taylor, "Hello Taylor, did you want anything to eat?"

With his hands in his pockets, he walks over to me, "I need to tell you something…"

I hold my hand up, "No, you don't. There was no way you could have known he was up here so please don't beat yourself up over and we'll never speak of it again. Deal?"

Watching his face, I could see the relief, "Yes ma'am, that would be nice." Taking a step closer, "I heard what happened, I'm glad that you're all right."

Waving a hand in the air, "The man was too drunk to do any harm, but we did find some things out. It seems as if he's been using several different identities, he's delusional and he's been in town longer than we thought." I turn to face him, "He was here when Mrs. Hopkins was killed."

Placing his hands on the back of a chair, he studies me for a minute, "You think he killed her."

Drying a plate, I turn to look at Taylor and nod, "Yes I do. For some reason I don't think Jacob Woods had anything to do with that. And for Joseph to drop him off there and then come back is suspicious."

Crossing his arms, he nods, "Makes sense. But no proof."

Folding the dishtowel up, I turn the kitchen light off and join Taylor at the table, "I heard Jacob was awake, think I could talk to him?"

With a smile, he nods, "Tomorrow we'll go to the hospital. Have any other ideas?"

"Only one. I think Carson or whatever his name is, will try to get in the house again. I'd like you and Spence to be upstairs for the rest of the night."

"Of course." Smiling at me, he leaves the room and heads for the basement.

The phone rings and as I answer, I see movement at the back door, with a quick glance, I see that the bolt has been thrown, so whoever it was couldn't get in. Picking the phone up, I didn't have to say hello, "We didn't finish yesterday, so I'm back."

I didn't say anything, I was waiting for Spence and Taylor to come back upstairs, but right then Spence yells out, "Do you still have that laptop."

The shadow at the back door stops and then turns. I yell down the stairs, "He's outside, go out the back!"

Hearing the door in the basement opening, I go to the front window and look out. He didn't have time to drive away and I didn't see anyone in the front or a car, so he must have come through the woods. I call Max and let him know and hopefully he could get a few more men over here to look.

Taylor comes back into the house, "Spence and Noah are tracking him. I'll be right back." He takes

off down the stairs to the basement, I hear things
being bumped around and then Taylor returns with
what looked like a large toy.

Chapter 41

"What's that?" I nod at what he's holding.

"A drone. Spence and I have been playing with it. See this, it's a camera so I can fly this in the direction we think he went and hopefully, find him." His smile was a little contagious.

"Can I watch?"

If possible, his smile gets bigger, "You bet. Where's your cell?"

Reaching in my pocket, I hand it to him. He taps at the screen for a few minutes and then hands it back to me, "This app is the camera on the drone, when you tap it…" Which he does, "It comes up, this way you can watch but you can't control anything."

Taking my phone, I tap where he showed me and smile as I look at my beautiful hardware floor since that was what the camera was pointed at, "How far away can I be?"

"Doesn't matter, you aren't controlling the drone, just watching so you can be anywhere and see what the drone is doing."

"Oh this is wonderful! Who would have thought technology could do these things twenty years ago?" I think back to myself just a couple of years ago until Terry introduced me to a computer and now, oh what would I do without it?

Hearing a vehicle in the driveway, we both look out to see Max sliding to a stop. Going out the front door, we meet him at the sidewalk, "Maggie, are you all right?"

"Of course. I told you he didn't get inside. Now the men are going to see if they can pick him up on the drone and I can watch!" I hold my phone up and smile.

Giving in to my smile, the worry left his face and he smiles, "This will be the first time we've tried this. Let's get to work."

Taylor and Max discuss strategy before setting the drone on the ground. Taylor has the controller in his hands and with a smile, fingers the levers. The drone's little blades start whirling and with a little bump, starts rising.

Literally clapping my hands as the drone rises and then takes off toward the east, in the direction of Noah's house. Tapping the app on my phone that looked like a little bird, the screen fills up with the ground flying by. Oh this was so amazing.

Max and Taylor were concentrating on the large screen that was attached to the controller while I keep my eyes on my phone.

Finally the drone slows down a little and you could make out the ground and the surrounding area. I could make out Blackie, Noah's horse as it passes, then the top of the cabin. We catch up with Noah and Spence and pass over them as they walk carefully through the woods.

He hadn't had enough time to get very far, so I was wondering if they were checking the right direction. The drone keeps going until it reaches the foot of the mountain. It circles and scans the area for a couple of minutes and then heads back to the mountain, "Chief want me to check out the mountain?" Taylor asks before guiding the drone in that direction.

Max nods, "Yeah go ahead. I don't think he had enough time to get that far, but let's make sure."

The mountain starts off with ample tress and underbrush, but if you didn't know the area, you wouldn't know that there was a steep drop off on the north side that ended in a deep gulley.

The drone slowly takes in the side of the mountain, sweeping the ground slowly before heading a little further where it turned into the side of the mountain and a sheer cliff that went straight up.

"Wait back up." I had seen something. Taylor turns the drone around and slowly goes back down the mountain,"Right there." Taylor circles the drone and you could plainly make out slide marks.

"Take it over the side." Max tells Taylor, concentrating on the screen.

The drone shows the side of the drop off with more slide marks visible. Then it goes down the embankment and there, a crumpled mass of clothes. He had gone down the cliff.

Max gets on his radio and starts calling for the rescue team as Taylor calls Spence and tells him what we were seeing. The drone goes down further where you could see the entire body, there was no way he could have survived that fall.

I keep watching as the drone takes in the scene and then Spence and Noah were standing at the top looking down. They both look at the drone and nod before they start looking around the area.

Max finishes with making the calls and tells Taylor, "I'll get the ATV and go up, can you direct the team when they get here?"

"Yes sir." Taylor brings the drone back which takes a few minutes and then turns to me, "Cool huh?"

"That it is." I slide my phone back in my pocket and walk around the side of the house, sitting down at the patio table.

Chapter 42

As I think over what had happened, I say a prayer and ask the Lord that we can find the answers now. With a sigh I get up and head inside, stopping in the kitchen thinking of what needed to be done if anything and then remember that the room they had been staying in needed cleaning.

Climbing the stairs, I reach the room and open the door, I start to enter and then stop. They'll want to go over the room for evidence. So I stand at the doorway and look into the room. The TV was now on the floor, along with every picture that had been on the wall. Everything on the bookcase had been tossed to the floor and the table in front of the window had been overturned and broken. My hands go to my face, oh my, why do all of this?

Going back down the hallway slowly, I enter our bedroom and curl on the window seat, two cats join me, "Hey guys, where's Baby?" I see her tail coming from underneath the pillows, "I guess she's taking a nap." As the cats curl up in front of the window, I slowly stroke their heads, enjoying hearing the purrs they were emitting.

I see the emergency vehicles go past the driveway on their way up the mountain, not envying the job they were facing. Saying a prayer for their safety.

I slide down a little and close my eyes, just resting my eyes. Waking up to someone softly saying, "Maggie." I feel a hand on my cheek, "You're going to have a stiff neck if you don't get up."

Smiling up at my husband, I start to get and grab my neck, "Ow!" With help, I finally sit up and start rubbing my neck, "I had no intention of falling asleep." I see that all three cats were spread out at the other end of the window seat, eyeing both if us.

Max sit down beside me, "You know he didn't make it."

"Oh Max there's no way anyone could have survived that fall." A thought occurs to me, "Was he drunk?"

"We won't know until the ME is finished."

"I think he killed Mrs. Hopkins."

Max looks at me and then leans back, "Care to tell me your thoughts on that?"

Situating myself to a more comfortable position, "He dropped Jacob off and picked him up. He was in town at the time and a lot of what Jacob said just doesn't make any sense."

"Like what?"

"He had the names wrong on the photo he was looking at. He's too young to be the son of Mrs. Hopkins daughter and if memory serves me, she wasn't a fan of the ummm…male persuasion." I could feel my face heating up.

With a smile, Max takes my hand, "You're saying she was a lesbian."

Jerking my hand away, "Well yes, I think so. She never had a date or at least I never saw her with a boy, but she was very close to Elsie's granddaughter. You remember her, she pretty much stayed at the library and was a quiet girl."

Max is quiet for a minute before nodding, "I remember her. And now that you mention it, I think you may be right. Where did we hear that Mrs. Hopkins daughter had a child out of wedlock?"

I just look at Max until he nods his head, "A source, but not a totally reliable source and we both know she adds her own version to things. And she was probably covering for her own granddaughter."

"Yeah you're right and no I'm not going to talk to Elsie. May be a good idea to talk to Jacob."

Getting up, I stretch my back before I start pacing, "I was thinking on that." Turning to Max, "I'd like to talk to him alone if you don't mind."

"And why are you asking me, we both know that you're going to talk to him no matter what I say." Reaching for one of the cats, he gets up holding Felix, "Now we're going downstairs to see what we can find to eat."

Max carries Felix downstairs with the other cats following. After combing my hair, I join them in the kitchen to find Spence and Taylor at the dining room table with files spread out before them and both with their heads bowed over their laptops, "Thank you both for acting so fast today. Sorry it had to end this way."

They both raise their heads and smile at me, "No problem, we're glad that we may have an end to this. Chief, we've been digging into this man for several days now and keep getting the same thing."

"I know. Let's get his prints and run them, I have a feeling they're going to turn up more than three identities." Setting Felix down, he picks up a file, "Why are you looking into Mrs. Hopkins?"

Spence looks at Max, "Just something not adding up so I thought she may be into something."

"Hummpf." I start to say she wasn't into anything but Max looks at me and shakes his head.

"I don't think so. I've known her most of my life, she wasn't into anything." He lays the file back down, "Why don't you guys pack on up and go on home. I want to thank you for being willing to stay here and watching after things."

Both men look at Max and then each other, "Sure Chief, if you're sure you won't need us for anything else."

Max nods, "I'm sure. See you tomorrow and be ready to come back and go over the room upstairs. We may get lucky and find something."

Taylor and Spence gather their things before heading downstairs to get the rest of their belongings. It didn't take them long before they come back upstairs, each carrying a duffle bag. Setting them down, they finish packing their things then turn to Max, "Okay Chief, we're leaving. You sure now that you don't want us to stay longer?"

"Thanks Spence, but I think the threat is gone now. See you tomorrow and thanks again."

After the men leave and Max locks the back door, he wraps his arms around me and holds me tight, "And I'm glad the threat is over too. Then man was nuts."

I laugh and look up at my husband, noticing the tiredness, "Me too and why don't you go to the den. How hungry are you?"

Scrunching his face, "Not very." Looking down at me, "How about a tray with cheese and stuff on it."

"Stuff? Hum, I have no idea if we have any of that and speaking of which, we have a ton of food that has to be eaten pretty soon since we no longer have any more guests coming."

Letting me go, he opens the refrigerator and frowns, "Wow, how about we load most of this up and take it to the homeless or the soup kitchen."

"Good idea. I'll fix us a little something. Go on in and put your feet up."

Fixing a tray with cheese and crackers, some ham, olives, baby vegetables and dressing, I carry it to the den to find Max took my word and had his feet on the table, the remote in hand and his head on the back of the couch and was snoring.

Setting the tray down, I go back to get a couple of glasses of tea before returning to the den, taking the remote from his hand and sitting down. Fixing a couple of cheese crackers, I flip through the channels until I find a crime show and settle back.

As I watch the show, I go over the things that Carson/ Joseph/ Wright had told me and decide that probably none of it was true except that he knew the Carson's. Maybe he had heard them telling stories of the Cambridge's and decided that it would be easy to come here and spin a tale and try to get something that didn't exist.

Getting interested in the show, I figure out the culprit and then talk to the TV as they drag it out. After it was over, I flip the station to the local news, mostly to hear what the weather was going to be tomorrow but instead find out that a body had been found on the mountain cliff and that foul play was evident. "Well great."

"Well great what?" Max was awake and leaning forward to get some food.

"The news station just said it was foul play on the body."

Max stiffens, "Wonder where they got that little bit of information?"

Chapter 43

The longer we sit and munch on the food, the more agitated he gets, I finally mute the TV, "Go on, you won't rest until you find out who talked to the press. But there isn't going to be but a couple of men in the station at this time of night."

"No, but the one I want to talk to will be." Putting his shoes on, he gives me a kiss and leaves saying, "Lock the house up."

Hearing his truck leaving, I sigh before picking up the tray and taking it back to the kitchen. Putting things away and washing our glasses, I make sure the door is bolted, turn the light over the sink on and return to the den. Curling up on the couch with my Bible, I get comfortable before taking my Bible and letting it fall where it may. When the pages settle, it's in Romans and my eyes fall on Chapter 15, verse 13 catches my eye, 'May the God of hope fill you with all joy and peace as you trust in him, so that you may overflow with hope by the power of the Holy Spirit.'

Holding my Bible, I close my eyes and think of what the verse says. Yes, I trust the Lord and yes, He fills me with joy and peace and yes, I trust Him. And yes, I do have hope by His power and with that power I knew that He was going to give us the answers. I also knew that whatever the answers would be, I would be at peace with it.

Waking up to loud voices, I glance at the TV to see an old comedy on, with Dick Van Dyke, I love his shows. I watch the show, laughing and enjoying myself. The cats join me and settle on the back of the couch as another show comes on, I had seen this

one too, but they never got old, so I watch this one
too.

Hearing a key in the lock, I glance at the
clock and see that it was after midnight. Max comes
into the den and plops down on the couch, "Did you
find anything out?"

Rubbing his face, "I did and now Officer Trent
is on official leave."

"Trent?" Racking my brain for who Trent was.

"He's usually working the desk. Young, still
has peach fuzz and is biting at the bit to be a
cop."

Nodding my head, "Yes now I remember. He's
over anxious and that may be why."

Letting one of the cats curl up in his lap, he
starts rubbing Oscar's head, "Thing is he's over
anxious about everything and is going to make a huge
mistake one day. I'd like for him to go through the
academy again." He looks over at me and smiles, "The
State Police academy."

I grimace, because I had heard that the course
was brutal, "You must really think he needs
extensive training."

Nodding, "As he is now, he's going to make a
major mistake in arresting someone or be overzealous
about pulling that weapon out and I don't anyone
getting hurt, no matter what crime they've
committed."

"Has he been through the psychology part?" All
the rookies have to go through psychoanalysis before
they are let on the street.

"Yes, but he didn't do very well, that's why I have him behind the desk." With a sigh, he lifts Oscar off his lap, "I'm going to try to get some sleep. Are you coming?"

Turning the TV off, I follow Max up the stairs and wait for him to finish in the bathroom before getting ready for bed. When I come out, I find Max with all three cats curled up to his side. He had his eyes closed but was absently stroking Baby's head.

I climb into bed, careful to not disturb the cats too much and turn toward Max, "Now that Carson or whatever his name was, is dead, are you going to close the case?"

"What case? We didn't have anything on him but threats and mischievous behavior."

"I think he's the one that killed Mrs. Hopkins."

Max turns to look at me, "And why, pray tell, do you think that?"

Giving him my thoughts, he studies the ceiling for a minute, "Good point." Looking at me, "And what else are you thinking?"

"That I would like to go and visit Jacob, alone."

Having his grey eyes bore into mine was making me a little angry, but I try to control myself and wait to see what he was going to say. "Sure. I think he's allowed visitors now. But to be honest, I don't think he's going to talk to you." Finally giving me a smile, "I've learned the hard way to trust your instincts. Good night." Cutting the light off on his side of the bed, he plumps his pillow before closing his eyes and letting a sigh out.

Knowing he was tired, I keep my mouth shut and turn my light out. Pulling the covers up, I close my eyes and concentrate on the Lord. Quietly praying, I ask for rest for Max, for comfort for whatever family Carson had left, for peace and finally to give me the right words to say to Jacob.

Feeling a little weight lifting off me, I let sleep take over. But the sleep wasn't restful, I kept dreaming of Carson falling over the cliff, of Mrs. Hopkins and that the new interim pastor doesn't show up for Sunday services.

Opening my eyes, I give up on sleep and quietly get up, trying not to disturb Max or the cats. Grabbing my robe, I go downstairs and put the kettle on for tea. As I wait, I think of what I want to ask Jacob. First was why he was really here and if he really had a family relation to any of the Carson's or Wright's.

Pouring water over a tea bag, I take it to the kitchen table and sit down where I could gaze out the window. There was a full moon tonight so I had a nice view of the back yard and the soft lights we had around the fountain made the granite shimmer.

Letting my mind wander to all that had happened in the past week, I can't help but think there was something else besides a 'treasure' that had brought both men here. If had been just a treasure, why was Jacob here? It seems the only thing he had questions on were the Wright's and his relations. He never asked about a so called 'treasure' or if there had been valuables found when we bought the mansion.

I couldn't help wonder if any of what Elsie had said about Mrs. Hopkins and her daughter were true though. I've lived in River Oaks all my life and don't remember the Hopkin's any trouble with children. Maybe that was because Mr. Hopkins was a lot older than his wife when they married.

With the three identities the man claimed to have, I was curious to know what Noah was going to find out about him. In my gut, I felt that Jacob didn't have any idea on anything else that had happened. It was going to be an interesting conversation.

Shaking my head, oh this was enough speculation, I needed to get some sleep. Rinsing my cup, I head back to bed hoping for a couple of hours before Max gets up.

Chapter 44

Usually one of us is awake before the alarm and turns it off. But this morning, the alarm jolts both of us awake. Once my heart had calmed down and Max had gone downstairs, I get up and make the bed, much to the cat's objection, "Oh hush, you'll just crawl on the pillows again anyway." Giving each one a rub before heading into the bathroom.

Once I was dressed and looking presentable, I join Max in the kitchen. Fixing a glass of juice, I sit at the table where he was reading the paper, "Anything in there about foul play being considered?"

Max lays the paper down and turns it toward me. The first thing I see is the headline, 'Suspicious Death Has Police Worried.'

"Worried over what?" Pushing the paper back to Max, I didn't even want to read it, "What do you want for breakfast?"

Twisting his mouth a little, "I'm really not hungry this morning, so how about just cereal?"

I nod and get up to gather the bowls and a couple of boxes of cereal. As I was carrying it all to the table, there's a knock on the back door and I see Noah. Putting everything down, I open the door, "Good morning Noah. Care for some cereal?"

"No thanks. I just wanted to go over what I had found out." He sits down and I get him a cup of coffee. After he takes a sip he looks at Max, "Ready?"

Max nods, then says, "Something tells me this isn't going to be good."

Noah smiles, "Let's say interesting." He straightens the papers he was holding, "I know you can't use anything I find and since he's dead this is more just information. First his real name as far as I can tell from the fingerprints I managed to get from the room upstairs is William Forest. He's has no ties to anyone in River Oaks and never has. He has seven alias' and he chooses the names from information he gets on families that have lost most of their descendants and that had a substantial amount of wealth, whether it was money, property or businesses. Anyway, what he did was to move to the town that he had someone marked and pretended to be a distant relative." He turns to me, "He wasn't related to any of the Wright's or Carson's that was a cover to get information on the available wealth. So he had come here posing and working to get the information and then left and waited. He also said he was a Carson several years later from what I can tell and tried then to get involved but James Carson wasn't a dummy and stopped him." He looks at us, "Good so far?"

I nod at him, but Max had a question, "How did he find out about these families? Just information he got in newspapers or through records?"

"I'm not sure, but I would think maybe from obituaries and I have a feeling, from town gossip. He's moved quite a bit so it's possible he moves to a town and hears some talk and then starts his little scam." He flips a couple of pages, "Okay, he was an accountant which made it even easier to get into accounts, I did do some research on an account that had several million dollars and was able to trace it back to one Silas Morgan. He had several businesses on the coast, seafood processing, a textile plant and a small printing company. He had no family and left the proceeds to the town and several charities. But I found a trail that moved some of the money to Forest's account. Not enough to raise any flags, only $9500 at a time."

"So moving that amount wouldn't alert the IRS?" Max was hanging onto every word.

Noah nods, "Yes. He had been arrested several times for larceny and embezzlement but got off each time. His lawyer is Robert Couch and he appears to be able to maneuver the charges down to misdemeanors." Lining the papers up before laying them down, "So that's what I was able to find, of course there is probably more but this was enough to let us know that he wasn't any kind of relation to anyone here."

"Thanks for working so hard on this Noah. We appreciate it." I pat his hand and he smiles.

"You know I enjoy doing this. Now, Jacob Woods, he's clean as far as I can tell. There isn't anything on him, those newspaper articles you read? All speculation. There was no evidence, no reason and there was no connection between Jacob and the lawyer that accused him. But…that same lawyer works with Robert Couch if that gives you any clue. I'd say Forest is the one that gave the insulin shot and blamed Jacob."

Max and I look at each other and I smile, "I didn't think he had that in him and I still don't think he had anything to do with Mrs. Hopkins death." I get up to finish cleaning the kitchen as Noah gathers his things up.

"Well that's all I have. If you need anything else, let me know." With a nod, he leaves, shutting the door behind him.

I turn to Max, "That makes me feel better to know that is wasn't a relative of the Carson's, I'd hate to think a relative would act like that man did."

Max folds the newspaper up and tucks it under his arm, "Are you going to see Jacob? Remember he hasn't talked to anyone so you may be wasting your time."

Turning to face him, "I have a feeling he'll talk to me."

"Oh you aren't going to unleash Margaret on him are you? Remember he's recovering from a really bad fall."

Laughing, I smack at him, "No, at least not yet." Giving him a kiss on the cheek. "I hope you have a good day."

He waves the paper, "I'll have to deal with this. So it probably won't be good." Picking his cell up, he leaves me to finish cleaning.

I think over what Noah had told us and with that information, things fit better. From his attitude, his actions, the reason he got here early to get more information. The only thing I was still wondering about was his connection to Jacob Woods, but hopefully I would find out today the reason.

Making sure there food for the cats, I grab my bag and leave the house and glad that there wouldn't be anyone rummaging around in it.

Chapter 45

Driving down the mountain, I think of what I wanted to talk to Jacob about and was almost to the hospital when I looked at the clock and realized I couldn't see him for another two hours. So I stop at the church.

Going inside the church, I hear laughter. In the office I find Betty, Mrs. Turner and Pastor Ross. They were sitting at the large round table, enjoying coffee, donuts and it appears, a good time.

When they see me, Pastor Ross gets up. With a warming smile he holds his hand out and says, "Margaret, so good to see you!" Taking my hand, he motions toward the table, "Please join us."

Noticing that everyone had an open Bible in front of them, "Oh my, did I interrupt a Bible Study?" I start to get up.

"No, no…we were discussing a sermon series. I would like to start in Romans, that's always been a favorite book of mine." Pastor Ross definitely had a winning smile.

Betty smiles at me, "With the outline he's giving us, I think we'll let him take us on a new path down the Roman road." She smiles at her own quip which made me smile.

Mrs. Turner looks at me, "I don't mean to change the subject, but can you enlighten us on what happened at the mountain?"

Pastor Ross clasps his hands together on the table and leans forward a little, "I've been hearing that you're quite the sleuth. Also a police consultant, how exciting!"

Betty gives a laugh, "Yes she is! She's help solve quite a few mysteries around town and she's also gotten involved in a few." She lays a hand on my arm, "Can I tell him about the cross?"

My family had given the church quite a bit of gold articles and one had been the cross that hung in the sanctuary, when pieces went missing, I found them under the baptismal in a hidden basement room along with a treasure trove of other valuables. The cross was now hanging back in the sanctuary and the gold communion service was proudly displayed in a glass case.

Patting her hand, "Of course."

As Betty told the story with Mrs. Turner helping, I blush a little at some of the things they said about me, but they definitely had the pastor's attention.

When they finish, he looks at me, "That's amazing. The story is of course, but that your family had built this church and then the gold? It's an honor to meet you and to know the history of this church. Oh what a history. Do you think we could meet one day and you could tell me more?"

"Well of course, it would be a pleasure. Although I don't know how much of it is amazing."

He chuckles, "From what I hear, just about everything you do is amazing."

"You should have met her several years ago when she was basically a shrew." Betty smiles at me while I give her a glare, "Well she still can be at times."

With that, I let it go and turn my attention back to the pastor, "I'm looking forward to Sunday, I'm sure you'll win everyone over."

"I have a good feeling about this and the church. My wife already loves the town and the girls have made a couple of friends. To be honest we're looking forward to calling this home for a while."

"Margaret have you heard anything else about Tom?" Mrs. Turner asks.

"Not for a few days. The last time I talked to Doc he said he was making a little improvement, but it was going to take time. To be honest the way Tom was the last time I saw him, I have doubts he'll ever be the same."

"That's sad. He's been a rock in this church for years." Mrs. Turner shuts her Bible.

Pastor Ross looks at each of us and sees the sad looks, "Let's pray for him, shall we?"

We all nod and then clasp hands as the pastor says a moving prayer for Tom and the church, the congregation, the town and for peace, "Lord I ask these things in your name and we ask to bless this town and church for the things that are to come." We have a moment of silence, "Amen."

Tears had formed in my eyes and I notice that Betty and Mrs. Turner were wiping at their eyes too, laughing I say, "Oh my, what a bunch of softies we are."

Pastor Ross smiles, "No, I'd call it Christian love and faith." Rising he looks at me, "I'm looking forward to meeting with you Margaret and I'll see you all Sunday."

We leave the pastor to his sermon preparation and go out to the parking lot where Betty stops me, "They weren't giving many details on the news report about the man they found, but was that your guest?"

Thinking really quickly on how much I should tell her and then decide a little information wouldn't hurt, "Yes he was. I didn't get a chance to talk to him much, but he was interested in the history of the area." I didn't elaborate that he was interested in the history of the mansion and the rumors of a treasure.

"Oh how sad, he must have been looking around the property and didn't know about the cliff." She shakes her head, "Such a tragedy. Well I'll see you Sunday." With a smile they get into Betty's car and leave.

Getting into my car, I sit and think about what people are thinking about finding him dead at the cliff. Years ago, I would have been a prime suspect, just from my attitude that everyone hated, "Oh Margaret, how far you have come."

Starting the car, I head for the hospital and then stop at a fast food drive thru and get two lunches. Parking at the hospital, I see the reporter for the local paper and decide I'd enter through the side, hoping to avoid them.

Moving my car to the side, I enter the hospital and walk to the reception desk. Thank goodness that Claire was working. She was a member of the church and I have known her since she was a baby, "Hello Claire. How are you?"

"Hi Margaret. I'm doing well, how about you?"

"I'm fine. I'd like to see Jacob Woods, Max said he was awake and in a private room now."

She checks the records and nods, "Yes he has. He's in room 422, you can go on up. And have a good day."

"Thank you and you too."

Taking the elevator to the fourth floor, I exit and find the room to see that Max had stationed a guard on the door. Since Carson, or whoever he was, is gone, why the guard?

Approaching the room, the officer looks up and smiles, "Mrs. Gunderson, chief told me to expect you. You can go on in."

Looking at his name tag, "Thanks Wilson."

Entering the room, I find Jacob with the bed raised and watching TV. From the look on his face, I could tell he was bored to death, I could also see his leg was heavily bandaged and was his torso, "Hello Jacob. Do you remember me?"

Chapter 46

He studies me for a minute and then his eyes change with a little smile, "You're the lady that owns the inn."

"I am. And I brought some food. I figure you're probably tired of hospital food by now." I set the bag and coke on the bed tray and sit down.

Pulling my own burger out, I eat, pretending to be watching the TV, but was watching him from the side of my eye. He finally pulls the tray closer and reaches in. He eats the burger in about three bites, I clear my throat, "How are you doing?"

Shrugging his shoulders, he keeps his attention on the TV.

"Have they said when you can leave?"

He shrugs again.

"Okay. You came to the mansion and had questions, which I answered. Now I'm here with a few questions and I would like the same courtesy."

He glances at me, then turns his attention back to the TV.

Finishing my lunch, I toss the paper in the bag before getting up and putting it in the trash can. Returning to my chair, I sit down and sip my drink. Setting the cup down on the end table, I lace my fingers and say a silent prayer before I turn my attention back to Jacob, "I assume you're aware that the man that brought you to town is dead."

His eyes flicker, but still doesn't say anything.

"I think he brought you here to kill Mrs. Hopkins and then when he robbed the mansion would blame you for that too."

His mouth tightens and I notice his fist clinching.

"So now that you are better, I'm sure that charges will be filed against you and without him, you may not have a choice but to plead guilty."

His head whips around at me, then he turns back to the TV.

Okay, I was tired of this, "Jacob, you seem to me to be a nice young man and I think that Forest coerced you in some way. But if you don't start talking and telling what actually happened, I can't promise that you'll walk out of town like you planned. Now I'm not the bad guy here, I'm trying to put the pieces together and with your help we can. But if you lay there with that mouth clamped shut and think that with him gone you're off the hook, you're mistaken. Now start talking or I'll go to the chief and tell him that you didn't seem too interested in helping yourself. It isn't any skin off my nose." I get up and reach for my purse.

"Wait." I look at him to see tears in his eyes, "It's not that I don't want to talk, it's just that what I know I don't think will help."

Sitting back down, I turn to him, "If it's the truth, it will help. Now please start from the beginning. When did you meet Forest?"

"If you mean Wright, it was several years ago. I was in foster care and my foster father worked for him. Well he did jobs for him."

"Was it your foster father that killed that young boy with insulin?"

He bows his head and nods, "Yes I think so. Wright could talk people into doing anything and my father worshipped him. He also thought that the more he did for Wright the more he'd be compensated."

"But it didn't work that way, did it?"

Shaking his head, "No, after everything came out about the murder, my foster father took his own life. Of course that wasn't in the paper and Wright walked away."

"Did you want revenge for your father?"

He shakes his head again, "Not really. He was a brutal man, nothing I did was good enough. He just wanted the money the state paid for keeping me and I overheard him say that more than once. After my foster father died, Wright wanted me to take over his work and I wouldn't do it so he said I owed him. By then I was 18 and legal so he couldn't really make me, he hounded me for a couple of years, he even said that I had something to do with that kid, which I didn't, then he offered me a substantial amount of money for what he said, one easy job."

"Coming here."

Nodding, "I didn't really know what he wanted, just to find out if some people named Carson really had a mansion and to find out as much as I could. He told me that the lady, Mrs. Hopkins, had some kind of proof that he was related and wanted me to break in and get it." His eyes turn to me, pleading, "But I didn't kill her, I couldn't do that."

Patting his hand, "I know. He killed her and
tried to shift the blame on you. But using the
insulin in the same way as that young boy, to me,
made it clear he was behind it."

Giving me a half smile, "Thanks. Anyway, I did
break in, but it was after she was dead, I didn't
find anything but I did stay there for a while after
the police left. They scared me when they came back
and I hid in the attic. Guess it was kinda dumb for
me to think I could jump out of that window."

I smile, "Just a little. What else can you
tell me about him?"

Frowning, he picks at the covers, "I know he's
pretended to be other people to get money from the
families. I know he's claimed to be a relative of
people that have died. That's why I'm here, he
wanted me to pretend I was the son of some woman
that had left here years ago and then he asked me to
pretend to be related to the Wright's." He looks at
me, "I don't even know who they are."

"The mansion was originally owned by a family
named Cambridge, there were several generations that
had lived there. There also was a family named
Wright, they more or less were caretakers and helped
in the office. I know that a descendant had worked
for my father for a while. But the mansion? It's
free and clear, Forest had no way to get a claim on
anything and the treasure he was talking about? The
Cambridge's had created a hybrid rose that they
called the 'Cambridge Rose' and it's beautiful. It's
won several awards in flower shows, but as far a
monetary value," I shake my head, "There isn't any."

His hands were in fists again, "So he told me
all this stuff about being a distant relative and

that he just found out he was left a substantial payout and that I needed to say I was related too, for what? He was conning all these people." Putting his head back and rubbing his hands over his face, "I wish I could go back in time and turn him in sooner."

"Jacob." I think of the best way to say this, "There was no way you could have known for sure about his motives. And I think if you had questions, he may have harmed you like he did the woman he paid to pretend to be his wife."

His head whipped to me, "What?"

Chapter 47

Just then, there's a knock on the door, I look up to see Max standing in the doorway. "Max, Jacob and I were talking and I believe a few things he knows may help."

Turning to Jacob, "Jacob this is Chief Gunderson, he's also my husband but please talk to him and tell him what you told me." I pat his hand and I stand up, "I promise it'll be all right, otherwise he has to deal with me." I start to leave the room.

"Wait, please stay." He looks at Max and I could see the worry in his eyes, "Is that okay?"

Max smiles and nods, "Yes of course. Do you want me to ask questions or would you rather just tell me the relation between you and Forest?"

Jacob looks at me and I nod, he starts talking and I sit in the chair across the room and listen. He pretty much told Max everything he had told me.

Jacob looks at me, "Can you tell me about the woman that he hired?"

Max turns to me and I nod, letting Max take over, "He had hired an actress to pretend to be his wife. She was drugged when she questioned what he was doing. We got her to the hospital and she's fine now. Did you know her?"

Shaking his head, "No, I didn't know he'd brought someone with him." He looks at Max and then me, "He's done that before, in Lexington. He was trying to get the title to a historical house, I was to be his son and he hired a woman to be his wife. After he got a few family heirlooms, the woman disappeared and he sent me home. But the funny thing is she left all of her stuff. Who does that?" He looks at Max, "I always thought he killed her."

Closing my eyes, I pray that wasn't the case, then look at Jacob, "Maybe you can give Max some information, the name she was using, what she looked like, where you met her."

Jacob nods, "Anything."

Max gets up and holds his hand out to Jacob, "Son thank you for talking to me, I know you've been coerced into doing these things, so no charges will be filed against you. And once they release you, you can stay with us until you're able to get around on your own." He nods to Jacob's leg, "It may be a while before you can walk without crutches."

A blush settles on Jacob's cheeks, "Thank you, but I should be okay."

Max gives me a wink before he leaves and I settle back into the chair beside the bed. "You did a good job."

Giving me a little smile, "I kinda feel better too."

"Holding all that inside was really tearing you apart. And now that you've confessed to what you've done, peace will follow."

He studies my face for a minute, "You're a Christian aren't you?"

Smiling, I nod, "Yes and might I add, very proud of it." I tell him my story of being the grouchy, argumentative, pain in the rear and then Terry came into my life and opened my eyes. I asked forgiveness and felt my faith come back and my life has been a complete turn around and I was happy, "Jacob, all it takes is asking forgiveness and believing that Christ died for you, you'll have everlasting life and trust me, a much richer one."

He watched my face the entire time I talked and I could see that he knew I was telling the truth and that he still had a chance at a better life. "Thank you."

Standing, "Well I think you need to rest now and I'm sure you have a lot to think about." Then I had a thought, "Wait just a minute." I go into the hall and walk to the nurses' station, "Can I trouble you?" She nods, "Do you by chance have a Bible you could let Jacob Woods borrow?"

The nurse smiles and opens a drawer, "By chance I do. It was left behind by a patient and he said to pass it on."

Thanking her, I take the Bible into Jacob's room, "Here, this will help. May I suggest you start in Matthew and then browse wherever you like."

He holds the Bible and smiles, "Thank you."

With a smile and a pat on his hand, I leave the room and make my way back downstairs. When I reach the front doors, I see the reporter still sitting outside, so I take the side entrance and get back in my car. Sitting for a minute thinking about what Jacob had said and then say a prayer that he finds his way to Jesus.

Chapter 48

Returning to the mansion to find Spence waiting for me, when I park and get out of my car, I walk over to him, "Hello Spence, what brings you by?"

"Chief asked me to get Forest's things out."

"Thank goodness, let's go clean that room out." Unlocking the back door, we head to the stairs and within fifteen minutes had everything packed and back downstairs. "Thank you Spence, that was a help and I'm glad his things are out of the house now."

"I enjoyed staying here. You have a really great place here."

Smiling, I look around, "We do. But I think this did it as far as me wanting to make it an inn."

Spence laughs, "I understand that one. Thanks Margaret."

He loads the luggage in his car and leaves while I go back inside the house and grab cleaning supplies before going upstairs to clean the room. Stripping the bed and tossing the bedclothes in the hallway, I wipe down the doors and knobs, the dresser tops, the light switch, any and everything that the man could have touched. I look at the painting he had pulled off the wall. The frame was hopeless but the print was still fine, so I roll it up to have reframed.

Standing in the middle of the room, I let my gaze run over everything and decide I cleaned everything, then I notice the TV and the large crack in it. "Well that's just great. A TV barely a week old and destroyed. Me and my bright ideas." Shaking

my head at myself, I pick everything up and go back
downstairs.

Loading the washing machine, I start the load
then put all the cleaning supplies up. Opening the
refrigerator, I stand and gaze at all the food
before deciding that chicken breasts for dinner
would be good. Pulling them out, I fix a marinade
and pour over the breasts before putting them back
in the refrigerator. I was definitely going to clean
the extra food out and take it to the shelter. There
was no way we could eat all of this before it goes
bad.

Hearing a car, I go outside to the patio to
see Max coming around the side of the house. He
smiles when he sees me then gives me a big hug, "You
were great today and thank you."

"All I did was talk to him. He wanted to get
all that off his chest."

"We've called Lexington and told them our
suspicions, they said they would start looking into
it and if they found anything would get back to us."

We head inside and while Max takes his coat
and boots off, I fix us both glasses of tea. Sitting
at the kitchen table, we discuss the day and what
Jacob had told us.

"There's only one thing that bothers me."

Max smiles, "And what would that be?"

"Why kill Mrs. Hopkins?"

Turning his glass around, he takes a breath,
"We may never know the real reason, but I do think
he believed she was a relation and had something

valuable." He looks at me, "It's sad, I know, but we have her killer and she's in a much better place now."

"I know, but it's still sad that she had to go that way."

Taking my hand, "Let's pray." He says a prayer asking for peace for Mrs. Hopkins, for glory and for understanding. For guiding Jacob and hopefully for him finding Jesus.

I open my eyes and smile at my husband, "Thank you."

"Okay. What's for dinner?"

"Chicken, potatoes, green beans and bread. That suit you?"

Rubbing his stomach, "It does at that. When are we eating? There's a game on…"

Waving my hand at him, "Go ahead, I'll wake you when dinner is ready."

With a laugh, he goes into the den and a moment later I hear the TV. Pulling the chicken out, I slide it into the oven and then dice the potatoes and mixing butter and garlic with them, then put the beans in a pot to simmer.

Going into the alcove, I pull up our website and look at the reservation page and let a sigh out. No one had asked for reservations. I disable the site and when I hit the enter key, let a sigh of relief out. I could do a lot of things, but running an inn wasn't one of them.

Glancing in the den as I return to the kitchen, I smile when I see Max in his normal position, head back, remote in hand and snoring.

I set the table, fix the bread, check on the chicken and potatoes before sitting down. With my Bible in hand, I start to open it to find my verse but instead, John 3:16 runs through my head and I smile. Yes it was a favorite and yes I believed. Closing my eyes, I concentrate on the Lord and let the worries of the day wash away. I let the image of Jacob fill my mind and pray that Jesus works in him, letting him find his way. I imagine Mrs. Hopkins in heaven, singing praises and happier than she's ever been.

Hearing the oven buzzer going off, I get up and put the bread in the oven as I start putting things in bowls.

Setting the last of the food out, I go to wake Max up but he was standing in the doorway, "May I say you look more peaceful now."

"I shut the website down." I look at Max. "I really don't want to have an inn now. Do you mind?"

He comes to stand beside me, "No I don't. To be honest I never wanted to do it in the first place."

I smack at him, "Then why did you go along with me?"

"If there's one thing I've learned being married you, once you get an idea, to let you go with it because there is no way to talk you out of it."

My mouth opens to argue with him, but I clamp
it shut instead, because he was right. But I wasn't
going to tell him that. So I smile and sit down,
spreading my napkin on my lap then clasp my hands as
we say grace.

Chapter 49

The next morning, I wake first and stretch. That was the first good night's sleep I'd had since Forest invaded the inn. It had been quiet last night, with no phone calls, no discussing Forest or Jacob, no running back to the station and it was nice.

Getting up, I go downstairs and start the coffee and pick my Sunday school lesson up. Maybe I could get the gist of it since I hadn't even thought about studying all week.

Just as I open the book, Max comes in the room, placing his hands on my shoulders, "Now that was a good night's sleep. I'm glad we talked to Jacob, it answered a lot of questions. And I hate to say this, but I'm glad that's the end of Forest manipulating people."

As he fills his mug up with coffee, I realize that last statement he made hadn't bothered me.

Joining me at the table, he nods at the book, "Haven't studied any this week have you?"

"And when would I have time, what Forest ransacking the house, drugging that woman, trying to kidnap me, I mean really."

With a huge smile, "So you have a good reason. Why worry about it? You know the Bible backwards and forwards, you could probably teach them something."

Smiling, "Thank you for the compliment, but there always seems to be a different interpretation of the verses, depending on who's reading them. And sometimes I like to challenge them, so I need to be prepared." I start to open the book when he takes my hand.

"Why not just go with the flow this week and see what happens. You know they may appreciate you not voicing your opinion."

"Oh you're just a ray of sunshine this morning." But I wasn't going to let him know he was right as I shut the book and slide it away. "What would you like for breakfast?"

"Let me fix it this morning while you go take a long, hot bath." Getting up, he kisses the top of my head.

Taking my coffee, I go upstairs to our bathroom. Turning the water on in the bathtub, I wash my face and decide my hair would be all right without having to wash it.

After a long soak, with the cats playing with the bubbles, I get dressed for church and go back downstairs to find that Max had fixed waffles and bacon, one of my favorites.

We eat in comfortable silence, each with our own thoughts, mine running toward Jacob and his recovery, both physically and spiritually. After we finish, I send Max upstairs to get ready as I clean the kitchen, once I was done, I sit back down at the table and open the Sunday School book, just to take a quick glance at the lesson. It was going to be in Daniel, the fire pit. With a smile I close the book then feel a hand on my shoulder.

"Just couldn't resist." Putting his suit coat on, "Ready?"

With a smile and a nod, I grab my things and follow him out the door. It was a crisp, beautiful morning and I stop, raising my face to the sun and thank the Lord for such a beautiful morning. Feeling my hand being clasped, I look at Max to see his smile and we both stand under the bright sun and praise the Lord.

Getting into his truck a few minutes later, Max drives down the mountain slowly, enjoying the view. Reaching the church to find the parking lot almost full, Max finds a parking space near the back. As we walk inside to the fellowship hall, we say hello to a few people, a couple congratulate Max on setting things straight about Forest's death.

Once we were alone, I raise an eyebrow at him and he says, "I talked to that reporter that Trent gave his thoughts too. It must have been on the news last night."

Not having a chance to say anything back to him since we had entered the fellowship hall. The place was crowded, there was a line at the coffee table and one at the donuts, but I made my way there anyway. Managing to grab one of the last donuts just as the buzzer rings, letting us know that Sunday School was ready to start.

Entering the ladies classroom, I take my usual seat and get my books ready. But instead of Betty coming in, it was Pastor Ross. Setting his things down, he clasps his hands and smiles, "Good morning ladies. I asked to teach the class this morning and I hope you don't mind." Sitting down, he opens his Bible, but no notes, "Shall we get started?" We pray and then he starts the lesson.

Forty five minutes later, I was calm and peaceful, he had done a wonderful job of describing the story without embellishing. There wasn't on single time I wanted to argue with him.

As we leave, Betty pulls me aside. "Isn't he wonderful? I'm so glad he asked to teach this morning."

Nodding, "Yes he did a good job. I didn't feel the urge to correct him once." I smile which makes Betty laugh.

Entering the sanctuary, I go to our usual pew and set my things down, before turning to greet a few people.

Chapter 50

As everyone settles down and the choir comes into the room, I give Tabitha a hug, then smile at Terry and Joy. I lean back and think how fortunate I am to have such a wonderful family.

The choir sings the first song then Pastor Ross comes in and introduces himself before leading us in the hymn, 'What a Friend We Have in Jesus.' The sanctuary fills with voices and it was wonderful.

Once we finish the hymn, Pastor Ross takes the podium and smiles. He did have a wonderful smile. "Please excuse us this morning since we are doing things a little different. I would like to have prayer now, for those that are on our prayer list and for those that really aren't aware they need prayer." He takes a step back and closes his eyes, a moment later he starts, "Father, we are all sinners. We all need to work on our faith, our belief and our sins. We ask You to forgive us of the things we do that are bad, that are rude, that are not compassionate. We ask forgiveness for all of that, we ask that You continue to work in us, to continue to guide us and show us what Your plan is for us in this world. Lord, we have several people that need Your healing touch, that need Your hands to take away the pain, to help with family problems or financial problems. Lord, we ask that You walk with us in every step we take. We thank You for Your loving goodness, Your forgiveness, Your grace. Be with us today as we study Your Word, to learn and to carry You into the world. In Jesus' name we pray."

Opening his Bible, I notice that he didn't have pages of notes like Tom always did. He pauses for a moment before looking up. "We're beginning a journey through Romans this morning, it's one of my favorite books of God's Word." He walks a little as he speaks, "I use the King James Version because I like the language, the terminology, the passion. We're going to start at the beginning with Paul telling us about what to believe. About becoming a Christian, about being a Christian and that we have to have faith and hope in faith. Please open your Bible's to Romans and let's begin at Chapter 1, verse 1." He preaches through the first chapter and it made me think of things a little differently. A little more hopeful. A little more forgiving.

After he finishes, he prays again and then the Music Director leads us in another hymn, this one 'Faith in Jesus.'

Pastor Ross comes back to the podium and smiles, "I thank you for joining us today and thank you for being faithful in your journey with Christ. If you haven't given your life to the Lord yet, this is a time for you to come forward, to pray, to declare your love of Him."

Taking the three steps to the main floor, he opens his arms, "Please come."

Several people went forward and knelt on the steps in prayer. But I hear a slight commotion at the rear, turning I see Jacob. Nudging Max I nod and he looks back, turning to me he smiles then gets up. Helping Jacob make it down the aisle on his crutches. I join them when they reach our pew and together we walk to the front where Jacob bows his head and I tell Pastor Ross a little about Jacob. Laying his hand on his shoulder, Pastor Ross says a prayer then asks Jacob, "Are you ready to give your life to Christ? That you believe in Him, that you will follow Him?"

Jacob nods and I notice that he's unable to speak. I take his hand and squeeze it, which made a few tears escape his eyes.

"Welcome to River Oaks son, have you ever been baptized?"

Jacob shakes his head, still unable to speak.

Pastor Ross takes in his emotion and says, "We'll meet this week and talk. You can let me know where I can reach you."

"He'll be with us Pastor, at the mansion."

Jacob turns to me and smiles, then nods.

Letting the Pastor talk to him a little more, I step back with Max and we meet up with the kids. "Mom are you okay?"

I was ready to burst into tears myself. But I nod, "Yes I'm fine. I'm just glad that Jacob is finding his way." She gives me a tight hug, letting me go so that Terry can hug me, I hold on tight because if it wasn't for this young man, I probably wouldn't be like I am today.

As people leave the sanctuary, we wait on Jacob to finish with the Pastor. When he turns, Max goes to help him, clapping him on the shoulder, "You did good son, real good." Jacob smiles at him, "Do you have any bags?"

"No sir, just my backpack and I have no idea where that is."

"It's at the station. I'll bring it later today. So the hospital released you?"

"Well I asked to be let go, I wanted to be here this morning. Something was really pulling me, so I asked where you two went to church and was told about this. Everybody in town knows you guys."

Max laughs, "Oh do we have some stories to tell you. Come on, let's get you to the inn and comfortable."

In the parking lot, we decide it would be better if Jacob rode with Tabitha and Terry then trying to get into Max's truck, so we agree to meet at the steak house for lunch before going to the inn.

On the way, Max and I talk about Jacob and the journey he was ready to take. We were both happy about it and I had no problem with him staying with us while he finishes recovering. Max was in agreement with me and said if Jacob got bored, he would take him to the station.

We were quiet for a few minutes before Max says. "One more thing though."

"What could that be?"

"The diamonds. What do we do with them?"

I had forgotten about the diamonds, the treasure we had found in the fountain. "I have no idea. Yet." Thinking about what they meant to the Cambridge's and the note that had been left in the box, "We can either put them back, find out how much they're worth, give it to charity or the town, maybe the church. We'll figure it out. But I do know that they are not to be used for evil."

Taking my hand, "As long as no one else is after them."

"Oh Lord, I hope not." I actually shake a little at the thought of someone else coming to tear the mansion up for a treasure. Maybe we should just put the diamonds back and forget we even saw them. Or we could give it all to charity and make a public announcement about it. Well we had other things to deal with right now, like welcoming Jacob Woods and helping him heal, so this was a problem for another day.

Thank you for purchasing this book, I sincerely hope that you enjoyed reading about the Adventures of Miss Margaret and I'm sure that everyone knows a 'Miss Margaret'. I apologize if you find any grammatical or punctuation errors, no matter how many times a book is gone over and by how many different sets of eyes and even an editor, a mistake may be found.

For other works by L.G. Blankenship, please go to Amazon or click on a link below. And as always a review is greatly appreciated, independent authors live by those reviews and it gives us the incentive to continue writing for your enjoyment. Lana

<u>The Sam Fields Series</u>

Illusions

Wicked Witness

Lost Decade

Force of One

Misplaced Intentions

Fools Treasure

Relative Involvement

Crushed Dreams

Corrupt Hearts

Diversion

<u>Miss Margaret Series</u>

Chapter 1…Again

Chapter 2…Begins

Chapter 3…Reveals

Chapter 4…Decisions

Chapter 5…Secrets

Chapter 6…Journey

Chapter 7…Vows

Chapter 8…Adventure

Chapter 9…Renew

Chapter 10….Confession

<u>Grace Hanson Thrillers</u>

Watching Grace

Come to My House

<u>Coming Soon- Nighttime Series</u>

Nighttime Justice

www.ingramcontent.com/pod-product-compliance
Lightning Source LLC
Chambersburg PA
CBHW071409150726
48000CB00001B/234